EARTH
CARE

Also by Margaret Read MacDonald

Peace Tales: World Folktales to Talk About
The Round Book: Rounds Kinds Love to Sing
Look Back and See: Twenty Lively Tales for Gentle Tellers
Thai Tales: Folktales of Thailand (with Supraporn Vathanaprida)
The Girl Who Wore Too Much: A Folktale from Thailand
Tuck-Me-In Tales: Bedtime Stories from Around the World
The Storyteller's Start-Up Book

EARTH CARE

WORLD FOLKTALES TO TALK ABOUT

BY MARGARET READ MACDONALD

AUGUST HOUSE PUBLISHERS, INC.

LITTLE ROCK

Published by August House Publishers, Inc.
P.O. Box 3223, Little Rock, Arkansas 72203
www.augusthouse.com
Originally published 1999 by Linnet Books
First August House edition, 2005

Printed in the United States of America

10 9 8 7 6 5 4 3 2 1

LIBRARY OF CONGRESS CATALOGING-IN-PUBLICATION DATA
Earth care : world folktales to talk about /
[compiled] by Margaret Read MacDonald.
          p.   cm.
Includes bibliographic references and index.
Summary : a collection of traditional tales and proverbs from over twenty countries or
ethnic groups, touching upon both human and ecological themes such as environmental
protection, the care of other creatures, and the connection of all things in nature.
ISBN 0-87483-784-7 (paper : alk. paper)
I. Tales [1. Folklore.] 1. MacDonald, Margaret Read, 1940–
PZ8.1.E125   1999
398.2—dc21   99-29785

Designed by Abigail Johnson
Illustrated by Zobra Anasazi

ಌ

For Diantha Thorpe, editor and publisher,

who lays her all on the line year after year

to make these books come true.

Contents ❧

An asterisk marks titles formatted by Margaret Read MacDonald for easy storytelling.

Introduction ❧

While working on my collection *Peace Tales: World Folktales to Talk About,* I began to keep a folder of stories about our relationship to the Earth. In the years since then I have read through many folktale collections, searching always for those stories which would speak pointedly to us. I found collections of nature tales already available for readers. But while many of these have fine stories about plants and animals, only a few of those tales seemed to focus on the problems in our relationship with nature.

In selecting material for this book, I chose only stories that make specific points. Harvest wisely, take care of the land, do not pollute, respect all life, seek the balance in nature, believe you can make a difference—these are a few of the themes you will find addressed in story here.

Several more fine tales that could not be included in this book are listed on page 143. And you will find a bibliography of other folktale collections on ecological themes on page 141.

Our most serious concern today is the preservation of this planet. Each of us must do whatever we can to help. Share these stories and help others think about ways in which our human actions affect all life.

All the flowers of all the tomorrows
are in the seeds of today.
—A CHINESE PROVERB

CARING FOR OUR LAND

Three Green Ladies 🍃

I open this collection with a tale of our responsibility to the land. The farmer in this story sees himself as a mere steward of the land during his lifetime. His job is to preserve it well and pass it on to the next generation.

On a hill in England there once stood three huge trees.
Those trees were hundreds and hundreds of years old.
No one knew for certain just how old they might be.

The farmer on whose property they stood thought of them
as being in his care for his life span.
He never spoke of owning the land.
He spoke of taking care of the land.
"This land is my responsibility," he said.
"During my life I will care for it the best I can.
As my father did before me
and his father before him.

And after I am gone,
my sons will care for this land."

Now there was a custom in this family.
Every year on Midsummer Eve
the head of the family would climb the hill with a fistful of
primroses from the garden.
He would place a few flowers at the root of each huge tree.
The farmer had done this every year
and his father before him
and his father before him.
It was a family tradition.

When this farmer was dying
he spoke to his sons.
"Remember to care well for this land.
It is your responsibility now
as it was mine during my life.
And don't forget to take a bit of primrose to the
Three Green Ladies on Midsummer Eve."

When the father died, the eldest son inherited most of the land.
To him went the huge farm and the hill with the Three Green
        Ladies.
To the second son went a smaller piece of land.
But the youngest received only a patch of rocky soil behind
        the hill.

As soon as that eldest son inherited the land, he began to brag.
"I OWN all this land!
Look at all that I OWN.
It is MINE to do with as I want."
He never said a thing about taking care of the land.

And on Midsummer Eve that son didn't set one foot on the hill
to take flowers to the Three Green Ladies.
"That old superstition.
Those old traditions should be buried with my father."

But the youngest son remembered.
He picked three small bouquets of primroses and climbing the hill
he set flowers at the root of each tree.
Then he sat for a while in the shade of those great trees.
He felt so comfortable sitting there in the presence of those old
    living things.

When he came down the hill his elder brother was waiting
    for him.
"What were you doing up there on my hill?"

"I was taking primroses for the trees,
  as our father taught us."

"Well, those trees belong to ME.
  I don't want you setting foot on my property again!"

"But I love to sit up there in the shade of those
  three great trees."

"Well, you won't sit there again.
  Besides, after tomorrow there won't be three trees there.
  There will only be two.
  Because I'm cutting one down for lumber to build a barn."

And the next day . . .
on Midsummer Day itself . . .
that elder brother climbed the hill with his axe.

And he chopped
and he chopped
and he chopped
at the heart of that tree.

And he chopped
and he chopped
and he chopped
at the heart of that tree.

And he chopped
and he chopped
and he chopped
through the heart of that tree.

And at dusk the tree was ready to fall.
But when that tree fell it screamed like a dying woman.
And a wind came up out of nowhere
and whirled that tree round on its roots . . .
and it fell . . .
on top of the elder brother.
And killed him there.

So the servants came and carried off his body.
And they sawed up the tree for lumber
and carried her away.

Now the second son inherited.
All the land became his.
And the two remaining Green Ladies were his, too.
But like his brother he bragged . . .
"All this is MINE!
All this property . . . it is MINE now!
I can do with it whatever I want."
And he never thought a thing about taking care of the land.

Next year on Midsummer Eve,
the youngest son again picked primroses
and climbed the hill to the Two Green Ladies.
He put flowers at their roots,
and sat for a while in their shade,
enjoying the presence of those old living things.

But when he came down from the hill
the second brother was waiting for him.

"What were you doing up on MY hill?"

"I was taking primroses for the Two Green Ladies.
Just as our father always did,
and his father before him,
and his father before him."

"Well, those Green Ladies belong to ME now.
So stay off my property."

"But I enjoy sitting in the shade of those two old trees."

"Well, there won't be two trees there after tomorrow.
I'm cutting one of them down for wood to build a fence."

And the next day . . .
on Midsummer's Day itself . . .
the second brother went up the hill with his axe.

And he chopped
and he chopped
and he chopped
at the heart of that tree.

And he chopped
and he chopped
and he chopped
at the heart of that tree.

And he chopped
and he chopped
and he chopped
through the heart of that tree.

And at dusk the tree was ready to fall.
And when that tree fell it screamed like a dying lady.
And a wind came up out of nowhere
and whirled that tree round on its roots
and it fell . . .
down on the second brother.
And killed him there.

The servants came and carried his body away.
And they cut up the tree for fence posts
and carried her away, too.

Now the youngest brother inherited all the land.
He looked on it kindly and said,
"Now I will care for you,
as my father did before me
and his father before him.
And my sons after me . . .
they will care for you, too."

And so he did.
He worked the land well and it prospered.
And every evening he would climb the hill
and sit for a while in the shade of the One Green Lady.

When he died his sons cared for the land after him.
And their sons after them.
And that One Green Lady is standing there still,
alone on her hilltop in England.

But I fear that one day soon
another young man will come to that hill.
He will take his axe and climb to the top.
And he will say, "All this is MINE.
I OWN it.
To do with as I want."

And he will begin to chop . . .
and chop . . .
and chop . . .
at the heart of that last Green Lady.

—A FOLKTALE FROM DERBYSHIRE, ENGLAND

Toitu he Kaainga,
    whatu ngarongara he tangata.

The land still remains when the people have disappeared.

—A MAORI SAYING

Treasure in the Vineyard ❧

Many variants of this tale exist. All suggest the same thing: In order for land to prosper, the farmer's eye must be over all.

There once was a farmer with three lazy sons.
There is nothing new in that!
This farmer worried about his vineyards.
He feared that once he was gone, the sons would neglect the
 vines.
He knew that the prosperous farm could easily fall into ruin.

Sensing that he was near to his death,
the old man called his sons to him.

"There is something I must tell you," he whispered.
"In the vineyard is buried a pot of gold.
It is buried within a foot of the surface,
so you should have no trouble finding it.
But I fear I cannot remember just where it is buried."

And without saying more, the old man passed on.

The sons worked hard that year in the vineyards.
They spaded here and there.
They spaded up the entire vineyard, in fact.
But they did not find the gold.
Still, because of their hard work,
the vineyard flourished.
The farm made more money than ever.

Understanding now what their effort could bring about,
the sons became fine custodians of the vineyards.
And the vineyards in turn
supported them well all of their days.

—A FABLE BY AESOP

 è•

It is the farmer's care that makes the fields bear.

—AN ENGLISH SAYING

The Farmer and His Crops 🐌

In this lively tale the vegetables require only a little help from the farmer, but he is too lazy even to give that.

The Hmong farmer made his farm far up in the hills.
With his big machete knife that farmer chopped down all the wild
    plants there.
He beat down the bamboos.
He cut to pieces the liana vines.
Those wild plants cried when he chopped them up.
"Don't do that, Mr. Farmer.
Leave us alone!"
But he kept right on working.
The farmer cleared out a nice garden patch.
He planted rice.
He planted corn.
Then he took his machete and went back down the mountain to
    his home.

That had seemed like a lot of work to this farmer.
He spent most of his time lying in front of his house napping.

After a while the rice and corn began to grow.
They grew and grew,
but when they were about as high as a roostertail,
the wild plants began to grow back too.
The bamboos began to beat at that corn and rice.
The liana vines began to wrap around the corn
    and rice to choke them.

"We don't want you, corn and rice," they said.
"You don't belong up here in the forest."

Poor corn and rice.
They jumped out of the ground and ran down to the farmer's
     house.
"You've got to come help us," they said.
"Those wild plants are trying to kill us.
That bamboo just beats us down.
And those lianas want to choke us."

The farmer was sleeping in his bed.
He did not like to be disturbed by these bothersome plants.
"Well, go back up to the field," he said.
"Tell those weeds to leave you alone.
Tell them I will come up one of these days and deal with them.
But I am sleeping now. Just wait a bit."

Rice and corn were relieved.
They ran back up the hill and sat down in their field again.
"You weeds had better watch out," said rice and corn,
"Our farmer is coming up here.
And then you will be sorry you bothered us."

The wild plants were a little bit worried at this news.
"What does your farmer look like?"

"Oh, he is very STRONG.
He will be wearing black pants.
And a black shirt.
And a black hat.
He will be smoking a pipe.
And he will be carrying a big machete!"

The weeds were distressed at this.
They backed off and left the rice and corn alone that day.

Next morning the plants all heard something
    coming up the forest path.
"I'll bet that is our farmer coming," said rice and corn.
"You are going to have trouble NOW, you weeds."
The weeds began to tremble.
But just then the path opened . . .
and a *tiger* came out.

"Is that your farmer?" asked the weeds.
"No. That's not him."
The weeds were relieved.
They started to choke at the rice and corn again.

Next day the plants heard something coming up the path.
"Here he comes now," said rice and corn.
"Just wait. He'll fix you weeds."

But the path opened . . .
and a *pig* came out.

"Oh, is THAT your big farmer?
We are REALLY scared," said the weeds.

"No, that's not him.
He must still be sleeping.
He will come soon though."

The weeds just laughed.
"Oh, SURE.
We are really scared.
He'll be here anytime now."
Those weeds began to beat on the rice and corn again.

Next day they again heard something coming up the path.
"Oh, HERE HE COMES!" cried rice and corn.
The weeds waited to see.
The path opened . . . and out came a *chicken.*

"Oh, SCARY," laughed the weeds.
"Is THAT your FARMER?
 We are really terrified."
And those bamboos began to beat on the rice and corn.
Those lianas began to choke them.

"Don't do that.
 Our farmer is really coming.
 He's just sleeping today.
 He'll be here soon."

Next day the plants heard something coming again.
"This is HIM.
 Just you wait, you weeds."
But the path opened . . .
 and out came a . . . *mouse*.
"This farmer is really going to GET us," said the weeds.
Those weeds laughed and kept beating on rice and corn.

Next day the plants heard something large coming up the path.
Rice and corn hardly dared to hope.
Had their farmer finally got tired of sleeping?
Had he come to take care of them?
"You'd better look out, weeds.
This might be him coming right now!"

The weeds weren't even scared anymore.
"Sure, anytime now.
That farmer is going to sleep all year.
HE won't save you."

But just then the path opened
and out stepped THE FARMER!
THEN those weeds were frightened!

That farmer took out his machete.
He began to chop down those bamboos.
He began to cut up those liana vines.

"Take THAT, you bamboo!
Leave my rice alone!
Here's for YOU, liana vine!
Stop choking my corn!"

Those poor weeds cried bitterly then.
And rice and corn cheered.
"Thank you, Mr. Farmer!
That is all we needed.
You just had to come look after us a bit.
Now we can do fine by ourselves.
You won't have to come up here again.
Just go down to your house and wait for us.
As soon as we are ripe, we will come to you.
But build us a little house to stay in at your place.
Just a little storage shed to keep us dry during the rain."

The farmer went back down to his home.
But he was so lazy.
That farmer just went back to bed.
He laid there so long his ear stuck to his head.
That lazy man.
He didn't bother to build a storage shed for his crops at all.

When rice and corn were ripe they JUMPED out of the ground
        and began to run down the path to the farmer's house.
Just like a river they ran, right down the mountain.
But when they came to the farmer's house they couldn't
        see their little storage house anywhere.
"Didn't you build us a little house to stay in?
Where can we rest?
We will get wet and rot if we have to stay out in the open."

Those crops just turned around and started back up the
        mountain.
"We only come to you once," they said.

"When you get your storage shed built,
    you will just have to come up and get us yourself."
And rice and corn climbed back up to the mountain,
    and sat down in their field again.

Since that day, the farmer has to take his baskets,
    climb the mountain, harvest his crops,
    and carry them home again.
So much work.
All because that one farmer was too lazy.

—A HMONG FOLKTALE

૨૦

Tay lãm hãm nhai,
Tay quai miệng trê.

If the hands work, the mouth has something to chew.
If they remain idle, the mouth will, too

—A VIETNAMESE PROVERB

CARING FOR OUR FORESTS

Beast and Tree ❧

This story shows the ecological disaster which can be caused by even a well-meaning consumer.

The tree was old
and beautiful.
Who knows how long it waited there,
content in dark
and proud in day.
Who knows how long?
Until Beast came.

The beast came snuffling, nose to ground.
It nearly rammed the tree before it looked.
Then, suddenly, wild GREEN!
Green light.
Green smells.
Green sounds of swish and sway.

"oh."
A small sound of awe.

16

And now Beast knew what it loved most.
Green.

Then *Crunch!* a fragrant mouthful.
Smunch! joyously another.
The Beast munched lovingly around the tree,
then wandered off to smile and sleep and dream
of green and leaf and tree.

Next day Beast hurried back
to lie against Tree's trunk,
groan sweet, adoring songs,
then round and *Crunch!* and *Smunch!*
and back to dream some more.

Here comes the beast.
Munch! Crunch!
Now back it goes.

Here comes the beast.
Crunch! Smunch!
There home it goes.

How happy are these days.

Till one day coming, habit now,
the beast can't find its tree.
It snuffles up. Down and around.
Nothing green here.
No scent.
No light.
No rustlings in the air.
Only an ugly stick
that whispers . . . "I need . . . I need . . ."

"Tree?"

"I need . . . I need . . ."

"oh."
A pang of dread.

"I took. I took from Tree.
I never gave one thing."

Now Beast is rushing to the waterhole,
scooping up mud to carry to the tree.
Packing good dirt around the poor tree's roots.
Then going for clear water from the stream.

Bring mud.
Bring water.
Leaves to mulch the roots.
No munching now.
Just saving, graceful acts.

Beast learned this lesson.
We might learn it, too.
If you will take,
You also must give back.

"I take . . .
I give.

"I take . . .
I give."

Beast's way.

—INSPIRED BY A FABLE
BY JAMES DILLET FREEMAN
AS TOLD BY JIM WOLF

૭ન

A man who kills a tree to feed his camel once,
deprives the herds of his fellowmen of food forever.
—A KUSHMAN SAYING

Who Is King of the World? ⁊

Here is the fable of an animal, who, like many humans, wants to dominate nature—in this case, one plant. "Beast and Tree", the previous tale, was based on this story. But it had passed through the hands of three tellers before I heard it. Notice how the oral tradition changes tales.

A plant and an animal once lived together in a small place that was theirs alone. The plant pressed its long roots down into the moist earth and thrust its long stems up into the warm air. The animal ate the fruit of the plant. This the plant did not mind; it produced its fruit in hope that it would be eaten.

So the two lived together for a long time, sharing their world.

But one day the animal fell to thinking about how superior it was to the plant.

"This plant," said the animal to itself, "does not show me the proper respect. It treats me almost as if it were my equal, and as anyone can plainly see, that idea is ridiculous. I, the animal, am strong and active, and this plant is weak and passive. I can move about freely and it is helplessly fastened to one spot."

So the animal announced to the plant, "Nothing is clearer than that I was made to be the natural ruler of our world. Henceforth whenever I approach, you will acknowledge my supremacy by bowing down and prostrating your stems upon the earth."

Now the plant was not a quarrelsome creature and was willing for the animal to consider itself superior, but to bow down and prostrate itself on the earth would be a hard and unnatural thing for it to do.

"The only thing that makes me bow down is a very strong wind," thought the plant to itself. "While this animal is a blowhard, it is certainly not a strong wind." So the plant continued to send its branches up toward the sun, which was its natural way of growth.

When the animal saw that the plant had no intention of bowing down and acknowledging that it was the ruler of their world, it flew into a terrible rage. It bared its teeth, flexed its claws, and let out a ferocious roar.

The plant paid no heed, but kept right on growing upright.

Then the animal shouted, "I'll show you who has dominion here," and fell upon the plant with tooth and claw. It hacked at the stems and tore at the leaves until nothing remained but a heap of broken branches on the ground.

The animal felt so pleased with its total demonstration of its superior power that it strutted back and forth, pausing only to roar occasionally so that the whole world might know who was the mightiest of all. That night, when it fell asleep, it dreamed happy dreams of dominion and contentment.

The next day when it awoke it was hungry and immediately thought about eating. It took a little while before it realized that its only source of food was now a rubbish heap upon the ground.

The animal ran from side to side in the place the plant and it had shared. But there was no question as to what had happened. It had torn up the plant that had sent forth the branches that had borne the fruit that had been its food.

Then it stopped strutting and it stopped roaring and it sat down dismally on its haunches. "I have made a very grave mistake," the animal said to itself. It lay down on the remains of the plant and wept that it had been so foolish and so proud.

Its tears trickled down onto the earth and watered the roots of the plant. For the roots of the plant were still there, deep in the earth, waiting patiently and acquiescently for their time to grow again.

The animal had hacked down stems and chewed up branches and leaves. But the roots of the plant grew deep down where the animal had no power to reach, and when they felt the animal's watering tears they began to stir in the earth and to thrust up new stems. The stems sent out new branches. The branches put forth new leaves. And in a short time the plant was heavy again with fruit.

But although the plant grew quickly, by the time the fruit appeared, the animal was scarcely skin and bones and its legs were too weak to hold it erect; it lay, an impotent huddle of hunger on the ground, helpless to lift itself up to grasp the fruit.

But the plant, swelling with new life, grew so luxuriantly and gave itself so freely that its fruit bent the branches clear to the ground so that the animal could eat.

When the animal had eaten and felt the life come coursing back through its emaciated frame, it realized how freely the plant gave of its fruit with no thought of holding back because of what the animal had done to it. Then the animal hung its head in shame.

"I had only the power to take life," it said to itself. "I can see now how little that is compared to the power to give life."

—A FABLE BY JAMES DILLET FREEMAN

Do not soil the shade of a tree that has been hospitable to you.

—A LAO PROVERB

Mikku and the Trees ❧

Here is a tale to help us think of the usefulness of our many trees.
See the tale notes for suggestions on using audience participation as
you tell this story.

One day Mikku went to gather firewood.
He could have walked into the forest and gathered fallen
    branches.
But that was a lot of trouble.
Instead he decided to just chop down the first tree he saw.

Mikku raised his axe and
CHOP!

But the tree screamed out.
"STOP! STOP!
Don't cut ME!"

"What . . . a talking tree?
Why shouldn't I chop you down?"

"Don't you see what kind of tree I am?
I am a BIRCH TREE.
You use my bark to make baskets.
You use my twigs to make brooms.
Don't cut ME."

"You are right," said Mikku.
"The birch tree is a very useful tree.
I won't cut you after all."

"Thanks, Mikku.
Remember . . . you care for us
and we will care for you."

So Mikku went on into the forest.
"Here is a good tree for firewood."

He raised his axe and
CHOP!

"Stop! Stop!
Don't cut ME!"

"Why not?"

"I am a CHERRY TREE.
I know you love cherry pies.
If you cut me there will be no more pies for Mikku."

"You are right.
I won't cut you after all, Cherry Tree."

"Thanks, Mikku.
Remember . . .
You care for us and we will care for you."

So Mikku went on into the forest.
Soon he found a broad, leafy tree.
He raised his axe and
CHOP!

"Stop! Stop!
Don't cut ME!"

"Whyever not?"

"I am a MAPLE TREE.
You make maple syrup from my sap.
And maple sugar too.
You don't want to cut ME down."

"You are right, Maple Tree.
I won't cut YOU."

"Thanks, Mikku.
You care for us and we will care for you."

Mikku went on through the forest,
but every tree had a good reason
why he should NOT cut it down.

Pine Tree gave its cones for Mikku's fires.
Cedar sheltered deer on winter nights.
Walnut gave its nuts.
Each tree gave something.

At last Mikku sat down to think.

"I'll just gather branches from the forest floor for my fire.
All of these trees serve a purpose.
It would be a mistake to cut any of them down."

No sooner had he uttered these words
than a little man jumped out from behind a tree.
The little man was such a strange sight.
He was wearing a coat made of birchbark.
His hat was made of acorns.
And his shoes were made of thistledown.

"Mikku! I see you respect and care for my trees!"
    said the little man.
"I want to thank you, Mikku."

And he handed Mikku a little wooden wand.

"Whenever you need something from nature,
    just show this wand and ask.
All of the birds and beasts will be glad to help you
    in return for your kindness to our trees.
If you want honey, show it to the bees.

If you want berries, show it to the birds.
When you are ready to plow your fields, show it to the moles.
All of these creatures will help you, Mikku.

"Just one thing, though.
 Never use the wand to ask for something
       that goes against nature.
 Never ask for something that should be impossible.
 NEVER do that."

Mikku took the little wand and went home.

"I wonder if this will really work."

He held out the wand and showed it to the bees.

"Bees . . . I would love to have some honey."

Bzzzzzzzz. "We'll bring it!" *Bzzzzz.*

The bees flew away.

In a moment they were back with a honeycomb
       dripping with honey.

"Why, THANK YOU, bees!

"Birds . . . I would like some berries."

"We'll bring them, Mikku."

In a flash the birds were back with beaks full of berries.
They dropped them in Mikku's bowl.

Now Mikku had life so easy.
Whenever he wanted something,
he had only to show the little wand to the creatures
       and they would help him out.

In the spring he took the wand out to the field.

"Moles . . . I would like my field plowed."

"We can do it, Mikku."

The moles dug up and down until the field was plowed.

Then he showed the wand to the ants.

"Ants . . . I have some seed to sow."

"We can do it, Mikku."

The ants scurried about and sowed all of the seed.

Mikku's life was easy indeed.

He became rich.
He became lazy.
And he became proud and boastful.
He got in the habit of giving orders.

One day in the middle of winter,
Mikku happened to be out in the field.
It was VERY cold.
The sky was cloudy and gray.
Mikku HATED this cold weather.
He was accustomed to having his own way by now.
Without thinking he held up his wand to the sky.
Mikku commanded:

"Sun come out from behind that cloud and shine on me.
I want to be HOT HOT HOT."

Hot sun in the middle of winter?
That is going against nature.
Mikku should never have spoken those words.

Immediately the clouds parted and the sun began to shine.
Its rays burnt down and Mikku grew HOT HOT HOT.
That sun's intense heat focused on Mikku and . . . *ZAP!*
Mikku was gone.

Nothing was left. Not even the magic wand.

Since that day the trees have never spoken to another human
being.
Though they say that if you walk through the woods and listen,
you can hear them whispering high up in the treetops . . .

"You care for us . . . and we'll care for you.
You care for us . . . and we'll care for you."

—A FOLKTALE FROM ESTONIA

&

Do not burn the tree that bears the fruit.

—A WOLOF PROVERB

Hold Tight and Stick Tight ᨠ

In this story the wanton destruction of trees reaps its just reward, while caring for a broken tree brings good fortune. Look in Japanese folktale collections for more stories about the kind old man and the mean old man next door.

Many stories are told of the kind old man and the mean old man.
In these stories the kind old man is married to a kind old woman,
the mean old man is married to a mean old woman,
and the two couples are neighbors.
And always the kind old man is very poor,
and the mean old man is very rich!

Here is one such story.

Every day the Kind Old Man would go in the forest to gather
   wood.
He would pick up branches and twigs that had fallen from the
   trees.
Then he would tie them in a bundle, and sell firewood in the
   town.

One day the Kind Old Man went deeper than usual into the
   forest.
There he discovered a huge old pine tree.
It was a marvelous being.
But some careless person had broken one of the pine's branches.
The old man heard the tree's needles rustling.
It seemed to be speaking.

"Ssaaap . . . ssaaap is drip-ping . . . drip-ping . . .
Ssaaap . . . ssaaap is drip-ping . . . drip-ping . . .
Pine Tree feels so ssaad. . . ."

"I can help," said the Kind Old Man. "I can help."
Quickly he tore off a strip from his clothing.
He reached up and tied the cloth around the broken branch.
He bound it firmly back in place.
"Now it will mend, Tree. Do not be sad."

All of the trees' branches began to rustle and move.
And high up in the tree he heard a voice:

"Hold tight or stick tight?
Hold tight or stick tight?
Which shall it be?"

"Well . . . hold tight OR stick tight.
Whatever you like, Tree," said the Kind Old Man.
He couldn't imagine what the tree meant.

Suddenly, round golden objects began to fall from the tree.
They stuck to the old man's clothing.
They covered his body from head to toe!

He could hardly move.
He was covered with GOLD COINS!

"Aaahhhh! Thank you, Tree!"

The Kind Old Man stumbled home clanking with coins.
His Kind Old Wife spent the evening picking gold from his
    clothing.
When she had piled up the coins, they were rich!

Of course it wasn't long before
    the Mean Old Man next door heard about this.

He hurried off to the forest in search of the magic pine.
After much searching, he found the huge old tree.

There was the branch that the Kind Old Man had mended.

"This is the place! Now I get RICHER!"

The Mean Old Man reached up and broke one . . .
    two . . . three branches!
"If mending ONE branch brings all that gold,
    just think what mending THREE branches will bring!"

But before he could reach to tie the first branch,
he heard a rustling in the pine above his head.

    "Hold tight or stick tight?
    Hold tight or stick tight?
    Which shall it be?"

"Hold tight AND stick tight!
Hold tight AND stick tight!
I'm READY!" shouted the Mean Old Man.

And sure enough, round golden objects began to hail down.
They stuck to his arms . . . they stuck to his head.
They covered his entire body!
But THIS was not gold!
The Mean Old Man was covered from head to toe with . . .
Globs of sticky pine sap!

"Oooohhhh. . . ." He was even stuck TO the pine tree.
Try as he might, he could not pull himself free.

And there he stuck for one . . . two . . . three . . . days.
One day for each of the branches he had broken.

On the third day the sun warmed the sap.
So the Mean Old Man was able to pull himself free and stagger
    home.

Out came his Mean Old Wife.
"Husband, where on earth were you?
Here you are with the GOLD at last!"

But when he came closer she saw that it was definitely NOT gold.
He was covered with globs and globs of sticky pine sap.

So the Mean Old Woman spent the evening
   pulling sap from her husband.

They say that kindness has its rewards.
Well, so does *unkindness.*

At least that's what always happens in these stories
   of the Kind Old Man and the Mean Old Man.

—A FOLKTALE FROM JAPAN

৯

Kindness is remembered, meanness is felt.

—A YIDDISH SAYING

Spider and the Palm-Nut Tree ❧

Liberian teller Won-Ldy Paye recalls this story from his youth. In his Dan village, taking care of the environment was the responsibility of every community member.

One evening, when the moon was full, the chief called everyone in the village together for a meeting. Someone was not following the rules of the village. There were rules for hunting, so that too many animals would not be killed, and there were rules for fishing, to give the fish time to grow. There were rules to protect the farms and the gardens and the people in the village, and there were rules about the trees in the forest.

This night the chief's main concern was palm trees. "Too many palm trees are dying," he said. "We need the palm trees for shade. The roofs for all our houses are made from palm tree leaves, and we use the stringy fibers to make ropes and mats and baskets. What would we do without palm oil for cooking and palm nuts to eat?"

The chief explained that palm trees were dying because people were tapping them to get the sweet palm sap. Beetles would go in through the hole and eat a tree from the inside and, after a year or two, that killed the tree. "So," the chief said, "from this day on, no one is to tap another palm tree."

Spider sat with the people and acted like he was listening to the whole meeting. But he was thinking, "Rules, rules, rules. I'm sick of all these rules. I like drinking palm sap. That rule isn't for me."

Very early the next morning, Spider sneaked out to the forest and marked several trees to tap. He cut sections of bamboo and made hollow tubes with sharp points. Then he gathered empty calabash gourds to hang on each tube for collecting the sap. Finally he tied reeds together to make a long ladder.

Spider worked all day getting everything ready. "Tomorrow I'll tap my trees," he thought. He could almost taste the sweet palm sap trickling down his throat. On his way home he walked backwards, brushing a palm leaf over his tracks, so no one could see where he had been.

The palm trees had been watching Spider all day. "I can't believe it," one said. "We give Spider so much, and now he wants our sap, too. He's going to kill us."

"I have an idea," one palm tree said. "I'm going to make sharp thorns that will stick him when he tries to get my sap."

"I'll shake him off if he climbs on me," said another.

"I'm going to grow so tall that he can't climb down," said a third. Each one had a different plan.

When the sun came up voices like a gentle breeze whispered through their leaves. "*Shhhh*," they warned. "He's coming. Spider's coming."

Spider set up his ladder and climbed to the top of the nearest tree, the one that had decided to grow. He looked around happily. "This tree is mine," he thought, "and that one over there, and the other one too." He was so busy pointing to trees and thinking about how smart he was that he didn't notice he was moving farther and farther away from the ground. The tree was growing taller . . . with spider in its top!

Suddenly the wind started to blow. That tall palm was swaying back and forth. Spider was swinging . . . swinging . . . suddenly he fell! But as he fell, he grabbed at a palm leaf and held on. Now Spider was dangling far above the ground. And then . . . the palm leaf split! Its fibers pulled apart and Spider began to fall jerkily toward the ground. Now Spider was halfway to the ground and hanging in mid-air, swinging back and forth. "Save me," he screamed. "I can't hold on much longer!"

No one came. But he heard a rustling voice quite close by. "Spider, you are stuck. I've grown so fast you can't reach the ground. If you let go, you will be very badly hurt."

"Who's that?" asked Spider.

"It's me, Palm Tree. Now hang on and listen."

"Can you help me?" begged Spider.

"I've been helping you all through your life," said the palm tree. "I have given you oil for cooking, a roof for your house, and nuts to eat. And you're still not satisfied. You went to the meeting in the village. You know that if you tap me it will kill me, but for a drink of sweet sap you're willing to take my life."

"Let me down," pleaded Spider. "I'll go away."

"If I let you down now, you'll just come back tomorrow to tap me and my friends," said the palm tree.

"I'm slipping," Spider said. "I'll do anything you say."

"Listen carefully then," the palm tree said. "I will make a deal with you. I will help you, but you have to take care of me. You have to promise you will just use the things that don't hurt me—my leaves and my nuts. And you have to promise you won't ever tap me again."

"I promise," said Spider.

"Then I'll continue letting down my thread," said the palm tree. "You can keep my thread. Use it when you want to climb on me again. But don't forget your promise not to harm me."

That was the beginning of Spider's web. He still uses Palm Tree's thread. And he never breaks his promise.

—A DAN FOLKTALE, TOLD BY WON-LDY PAYE
AND MARGARET H. LIPPERT

ॐ

Strong desire is the origin of pain.

—FROM THE *LOTUS SUTRA*, INDIA

CARING FOR OUR WETLANDS

The Tiddy Mun ⁊

A story of man's relationship to the marsh, full of magical elements and cautions. The story was told by an old woman who lived in the Cars of the Ancholme Valley in England in the late 1800s. She had performed these rites herself when young, but thought no one now even remembered the Tiddy Mun. He was called "Tiddy Mun" because he was so small, and had no other name. In this story people mourn for the mythical creatures of their marsh which are displaced when men try to drain the marsh and alter nature. I have kept much of the tale's unusual dialect.

A while back, before the dikes were made, and the riverbed changed, when the Cars were nothing but bog-lands, and full of water holes; they were teeming, as you have heard, with boggarts and will-of-the-wykes, and such like; voices of dead folks, and hounds without arms, that came in the darklins, moaning and crying and beckoning all night through; todlowries dancing on the tussocks, and witches riding on the great black snags, that turned to snakes, and raced about with them in the water; my word! It twas a strange and ill place to be in, come evening.

For were scared of them naturally and would not go near without a charm of some sort, just a witches pink or a Bible-ball, or the likes of that. I'll tell you about them another time. They shook with fright, I'll tell you, when they found themselves in the Cars at darklins. For certain, they were shaking in their time; for the ague and fever were terrible bad, and there were poor weak folk fit for nothing. In my young days, we all had the augue, the men out in the fields, even the babes had the shakes regularly. Ay maybe, things are better off now, but I don't know, I don't know. We've lost Tiddy Mun. Well . . . well. They understood fine that the fever and augue came from the bogs, but so come as they heard tell, that the marshes must be drained as the cause of it, they were sore miscontented, for they were used to them, and their fathers before them and they thought, as the saying goes, bad's bad, but meddling's worse.

They'd tell them fine tales, that the mist would lift, and that the bogs would come in the molds, and there would be no more augue; but they disliked the change, and were main fratched with the Dutchmen, who came across the sea for their delving.

The folk would not give the Dutchmen vittels or bedding or fair words; no one let them cross the doorsill; and they said to each other, they said, as it would be ill days for the Cars, and the poor Car-folk, if the bog-holes were meddled with, and Tiddy Mun was made unhappy.

For you know, Tiddy Mun dwelt in the water-holes down deep in the green still water, and he came out only in evening, when the mist rose. Then he came creeping out in the darklins, limpelty lobelty, like a dearie wee auld grandfather, with long white hair, and a long white beard, all clotted and tangled together; limpelty-lobelty, and gowned in gray, while they could scarce see him through the mist, and he came with a sound of running water, and a sighing of the wind, and a laughing like a pyewipe screech. They were not so scared of Tiddy Mun as of the boggarts and such however. He wasn't wicked and tantrummy like the water-wives; and he wasn't white and creepy like the Dead Hands. But nonetheless, it was sort of shivery-like when they set round the fire, to hear the screeching laugh out by the door, passing in a skirl of wind and water; still they only pulled in a bit closer together, and whispered with a peek over the shoulder, "Harken to Tiddy Mun!"

Mind you, the Old Man hurt no one, nay, he was real good to one at times. When the year was getting wet, and the water rose in the marshes, while it crept up to the doorsill, and covered the pads, come the first New Moon, the father and mother, and the brats, would go out in the darklins, and looking over the bog, call out together, though perhaps a bit scared and quavery-like:

"Tiddy Mun, without a name,
 Thy waters THRUFF!"

and all holding on together and trembling, they'd stand shaking and shivering, while they heard the pyewipe screech across the swamp; it was the Old Man's holla! And in the morn, sure enough, the water would be down, and the pads dry. Tiddy Mun had done the job for them.

What's that? Ay, they called him Tiddy Mun, for he was not bigger than a three-year's bairn, but he had no right sort of name—never had one. Someday I'll tell you how that happened.

So as we were saying. Tiddy Mun dwelled in the water-holes, and now that the Dutchmen were emptying them out, while they were dry as a two-year-old Motherin cake—and you'll not take much of that. Have you heard the old rhyme, that says:

"Tiddy Mun, wi-out a name
 White head, walkin' lame;
 While tha water teems tha fen
 Tiddy Mun'll harm nane."

And this was the bother! For the water-holes were most dried, and the water was drawn off into big dikes, so that the soppy, quivering bog was turning into form molds, and where'd the Tiddy Mun be then? Everybody said, that ill times were coming for the Cars.

But, however, there was no help for it; the Dutchmen delved, and the Dutchmen drawed the water off, and the dikes got ever longer and longer, and deeper and deeper; the water ran away, and ran away down to the river, and the black soft bog-lands would soon be turned to fields.

But though the work was getting done, it was not without trouble. At the Inn of Nights, on the great settle, and in the kitchens at home, they whispered strange and queer tales, ay dearie me, strange and queer, but true as death! And the old folk wagged their heads, and the young ones wagged their tongues, and the some thought, and the others said:

"Ay, and for sure, it's ill comes of crossing Tiddy Mun!"

For mark my words! It was first one and then another of the Dutchmen was gone, clean spirited away! Not a sight of him anywheres! They sought for him, and sought for him, but not a shadow of him was ever seen more, and the Car-folk knew fine, that they'd never find him, nay, not if they sought till the golden Beasts of Judgment came a-roaring and a-ramping over the land, for to fetch the sinners.

Tiddy Mun had fetched them away, and drowned them in the mud holes, where they hadn't drawn off all the water!

And the Car-folk nodded and said:
"Ay, that comes o' crossin' Tiddy Mun!"

But they brought more Dutchmen for the work, and though Tiddy Mun fetched on, and fetched on, the work got on nonetheless and there was no help for it.

And soon the poor Car-folk knew that the Old Man was sore fratched with everybody.

For soon he sneepit all in turn; the cows pined, the pigs starved, and the ponies went lame; the brats took sick, the lamps dimmed, the meal burnt itself, and the new milk curdled; the thatch fell in, and the walls burst out, and all an anders went arsy-varsy.

At first the Car-folk couldn't think that the Old Man would worry his own people such a way; and they thought mayhap it was the witches or the todlowries, that had done it. So the lads stoned the wall-eyed witch up to Gorby out of the Market-Place, and Sally to Wadham with the Evil Eye, she that charmed the dead men out of their graves, in the churchyards; they ducked she in the horse-pond until she was nearly dead; and they all said "Our Father" backwards and spat to the east to keep the todlowries pranks off; but it was not helping; for Tiddy Mun himself was angered, and he was visiting it on his poor Car-folks. And what could they do?

The bairns sickened in their mothers' arms; and their poor white faces never brightened up; and the fathers sat and smoked, while the mothers cried over the wee innocent babies lying there so white an smiling and peaceful. It was like a frost that comes and kills the bonniest flowers. But the hearts were sore , and their stomachs empty, with all this sickness and bad harvest and what not; and something must be done, or the Car-folk would soon be all dead and gone.

In the end, some one minded how, when the waters rose in the marshes, before the delving; and the folk called out to Tiddy Mun, come New Moon in the darklins; he heard and did as he was asked. And they thought, mayhap if they called him again, so as to show him like, as the Car-folk wished him well, and that they'd give him back the water if they only could—maybe he'd take the bad spell undone, and forgive them again.

So they fixed that they should meet together come the next New Moon down by the cross dike, by the old stoop next to John Ratton's field.

Well, it was a regular gathering, there was old Tom of the Hatch, and Wellem, his sister's son, from Priestrigg; and crooked Fred Lidgitt, and Brock of Hell-gate, and Ted Badley, that were father's brothers to me; and lots more of them, with women-folk and babes. I'll not say I was not there myself, just maychance you know it!

They came in threes and fours, jumping at every sight of the wind, and screeching at every snag, but they didn't need, for the poor old boggarts and Jack O'Lanterns were clean delved away.

They came, every one with a stoup of fresh water in their hand; and while it darkened, they stood all together, whisperin' and flusterin,' peekin' at the shades over their shoulders, and harkenin' uneasy-like to the skirlin' of the wind, and the liplap of the runnin' water.

Come the darklins at long last, and they stood all of them at the dike-edge, and lookin' over to the new river, they called out all together, strange and loud,

"Tiddy Mun, wi-out a name,
Here's water for thee,
take thy spell undone!"

And they poured the water out of their stoups into the dike, *Splash! Sploppert!*

It was scareful, standin' holdin' on together, in the stillness. They harkened with all their might, to hear if Tiddy Mun answered them; but there was nothing but unnatural stillness. And then, just when they thought it was no good, there broke out the awfullest wailin' and whimperin' all round about them; it came backwards and forwards, for all the world like a lot of little cryin' babies greetin' as if to break their hearts, and no one to comfort 'em; who sobbed and sobbed themselves most quiet, and then began again louder than ever, wailin' and moanin' till it made one's heart break to hear them.

And all at once the mothers cried out as if it were their dead babes, calling on Tiddy Mun to take the spell undone, and let their children live and grow strong; and the poor innocents, fleeing above us in the darklins, moaned and whimpered softlike, as if they knew their mothers' voices and were tryin' to reach their bosom. And there were women who said that tiny hands touched them, and cold lips kissed them, and soft wings fluttered round them that night, as they stood waitin' and harkenin'; to that woeful greetin'. Then all at once, there was stillness again, and they could hear the water lappin' at their feet, and the dog yelping in the fields. But then came soft and fond-like from the river itself, the old pyewipe screech, once and again it came, and for true, it was the Old Man's holler. And they knew he had taken the spell undone, for it was so kind and broodlin' and sorry-like as never was.

Ay dearie day! How they laughed and cried together, runnin' an' jumpin' about, like a pack of brats coming out o' school, as they set off home, with light hearts, and never a thought on the bog-garts. Only the mothers thought of their dead babies and their arms felt empty and their hearts lonesome and wearyin' for the cold kiss and the flutterin' o' the tiny fingers, an' the grief wi' thinkin' on their poor wee bodies, driftin' about in the sighin' o' that night wind.

But from that day, mark my words! It was strong and thrivin' in the Cars. The sick babes got well, and the cattle thrived, and the bacon-pigs fattened; the men folk made good wages, and bread was plenty; for Tiddy Mun had taken the bad spell undone. But every New Moon as was, out they went in the darklins, to the nearest dike edge, father and mother and brats; and they tipped the water in the dike cryin':

"Tiddy Mun wi-out a name
Here's water for thee!"

And the pyewipe screech would come back, soft and tender and pleased.

But the day is gone by, and folks now know nought about him. Ay, faith, it is true for all that; I've seen him myself, limpin' by in the fog, all gray an' white', an' screechin' like the pyewipe, but tis long since he's been by, and I've tipped the water out of the stoup too, but I'm too old now, thou see, and cannot walk, since years gone. But I guess Tiddy Mun's been frighted away with all the new ways and gear, for folk dinna know him any more, and you never hear say now, as we used to say when we were young, and anybody had a might of trouble and mischance, and wry luck, as said,

"Ah, thou haven't been out in the New Moon lately, and for certain-sure, it's ill to cross Tiddy Mun wi-out a name!"

—A FOLK LEGEND FROM ENGLAND

&❧

If a carabao with its four feet can make a wrong step,
how much more easily a man.

—A PROVERB FROM THE PHILIPPINES

The New Lake ❧

This ill-conceived "improvement" project of an ancient Chinese gov-ernment reminds us of some of today's governmental schemes.

During the Sung Dynasty, Wang An-shih was prime minister. He was always eager to start new public works projects. One day Lee Kung-fu came to court to promote a great new project.

"I suggest that we drain Liang-shanpo Lake. I, myself, will be glad to organize this project. Once the lake is drained we will gain eight hundred square li of fertile land!"

Wang An-shih was eager to begin at once on this new project. But something occurred to him. "Where will all of the water from the lake go?

"Oh, that is simple. I will handle that project also. We will just dig another lake of the same size beside it and funnel the water over."

Wang Ah-shih laughed and declined the project.

—A FOLKTALE FROM CHINA

❧

A fool always comes short of his reckoning.

—AN ENGLISH SAYING

Fox Rules the Streams 🍂

Fox here is the power-hungry administrator, bending nature to his own will. The brave little Pla Moo fish is the lone fighter for environmental needs. The story resonated among my students in Thailand, where well-meaning governmental dam projects spell disaster for many small farmers.

Once Fox was made supervisor of the stream.
He took this to mean that he could do just as he liked with the
    stream, its creatures, and all who lived on its banks.

The fish and other living things in the stream's waters were for
    HIM to eat.
The animals who drank from the stream were HIS servants.

One day Fox saw tiny shrimp swimming in the shallow pool where
    he was drinking.
"LUNCH!" thought Fox.

The shrimp saw at once that they must be clever to save their
    lives.
This pool was so shallow that there was nowhere they could
    escape.
But the shrimp made a plan.

Several of the shrimp poked their heads out of the water and
    began to flatter Fox.
"Mr. Fox, you are soooo beautiful!
Your fur is soooo soft and shiny!"

Fox stopped and looked at himself. He WAS beautiful.

While Fox was admiring his coat, the shrimp dove to the bottom
of the shallow pool and rolled themselves in mud.

Now they popped to the top.

"Mr. Fox, we can see you would enjoy eating us.

But look how MUDDY we are.

Surely you will want to wash us before you have your lunch."

"Oh, you ARE muddy.

I will wash you right now

and THEN I will eat you."

"Mr. Fox, you cannot wash us HERE.

This pool is too muddy."

"Then what can I do?"

"Come into the water and we will jump into your fur.

Then you can carry us downstream to a clear pool.

There you can wash us and EAT us."

So the fox waded into the stream

and the little shrimp all jumped into his fur.

The fox splashed downstream until he came to another shallow
pool.

"I will wash you here and EAT you, little shrimp."

"Oh no, Mr. Fox,

This pool is too muddy.

You must find a deeper pool."

Fox splashed on downstream to another shallow pool.

"I will wash you here, little shrimp.

And then I will EAT you."

But this pool was also too shallow for the shrimp to escape.

"Oh NO, Mr. Fox.
 The water here is too muddy!
 Go on downstream a bit."

Fox splashed on down the stream.
At last he came to a deep pool.

"This is the spot, Mr. Fox!
 The water here is clear.
 Wade right in and you can wash us and EAT us."

So the foolish fox waded in.
As soon as the water touched his fur, the little shrimp jumped off.
They dove deep to the bottom of the pool, giggling.
"Goodbye, Mr. Fox, thanks for the RIDE!"

Fox was furious.
"Those little shrimp!
 They TRICKED me!
 But I will show THEM who rules this stream!"

Fox began to call his servants from the forest.

"ELEPHANTS! If you want to keep drinking from this stream,
    get out here, RIGHT NOW!"

"PYTHONS! If you want to keep drinking from this stream,
    get out here, RIGHT NOW!"

The animals hurried to see what the Stream Boss wanted.

"Pythons, half of you go down below the pool.
 Stack your bodies up across the river and make a DAM!
 We will trap those shrimp right here!"

The pythons hurried to squeeze their long bodies together across
    the stream.
They made a strong dam and no water could flow out of that pool.

"Pythons, the rest of you go upstream and make a dam just above this pool."

The other pythons lined their bodies up and squeezed close together.

They made a strong dam above the pool.

Now no water could flow into the pool and no water could flow out of the pool.

The shrimp were trapped.

"All RIGHT!" said Fox.

"Now ELEPHANTS, slurp up the water and spit it over the dam!"

The elephants all dropped their long trunks into the pool and began to slurp.

They stretched their long trunks over the dam and squirted water out.

Slurp . . . squirt . . . slurp . . . squirt . . . slurp . . . squirt. . . .

Slowly the water level of the pool began to drop.

Lower and lower sank the water.

The little shrimp were hiding in the mud at the very bottom of the pool.

Fox still couldn't reach them.

But the fish in the pool were stranded in the mud as the water level dropped.

They were flopping and dying in the hot sun.

Now in this pool there was one little fish who was braver than all the others.

The tiny Pla Moo fish had a very brave heart!

Little Pla Moo saw that the stream creatures would soon all be dead.

"Fox is killing ALL of the creatures in this stream!

These fish will not live to have children.

Their generations will die out.

All of the creatures in this stream are going to become extinct!

One or two fish Fox may eat, yes . . . but he must not kill them
    ALL!
I cannot let this happen."

And that brave little fish began to squirm
    right between two of the snake bodies in that snake-dam.
He squirmed and squirmed and held his breath and squirmed
    some more and . . .
POP, he was out on the other side, swimming downstream in
    search of help.

Pla Moo swam downstream as fast as he could.
At every pool he would stand on his tail and call to anyone who
    might hear,
    "Chuay Duay! Chuay Duay! Chuay Duay!"
    "Help! Help! Help!"
But no one was around to help.

So he swam on downstream.
    "Chuay Duay! Chuay Duay! Chuay Duay!"

Still no one in sight.
On and on he swam.
    "Chuay Duay! Chuay Duay! Chuay Duay!"
At last! There was Rabbit nibbling by the side of the stream.

"Little Pla Moo? What is wrong?"

"It is FOX! He has dammed up the stream.
 The elephants are draining the pool!
 All of the stream creatures are going to die!
 They will never live to have children.
 Their generations will become extinct!"

"We cannot ALLOW this!" said Rabbit.
"I will help you, Pla Moo."

Rabbit left off his munching and began to hop back upstream.
Little Pla Moo struggled bravely upstream too.

Hopping and struggling, the two small animals at last reached the dam.

"Wait." Rabbit thought a moment. Then he had a plan.
Rabbit picked a large green leaf.
He rolled it around until he had made a shape just like a megaphone.
He hid himself behind a tree, and putting the leaf horn to his mouth,
Rabbit began to call:

> *"HAAAM POK!*
> *HAAAM POK!*
> Hit the head of the fox!
> Pull the trunks off the elephants!
> Tie the snakes into knots!
> *HAAAM POK!*
> The *YAAK* is COMING!
> The GIANT is COMING!"

"It's the *YAAK!*
It's the GIANT!
We'd better RUN!" cried the elephants and pythons.

But Fox ordered them to stay in place.

"Elephants! Keep on working!"
"Snakes! Don't you move!"
"I am the BOSS.
Do as I say!"

So the elephants kept on slurping. But they were trembling as they did it.

Slurp . . . squirt . . slurp . . . squirt . . . slurp. . . .

The snakes stayed in place . . . but they were nervous.
Those snake dams were beginning to wobble.

Rabbit came a little closer.

He called even louder, and the leaf horn made his voice boom out.

> *"HAAAM POK!*
>
> *HAAAM POK!*
>
> Hit the fox on the head!
>
> Pull the trunks off the elephants!
>
> Tie the snakes into knots!
>
> *HAAAM POK!*
>
> The *YAAK* is HERE!"

Now the animals were terrified.

"RUN FOR YOUR LIVES!"

Those elephants stampeded off in every direction.

The snakes began to writhe and squirm and the dam broke.

While the snakes slithered off into the forest, the water rushed
   downstream.

And with it swam the happy fishes.

Behind them swept the little shrimp, giggling,

"Goodbye, Mr. Fox," as they drifted away.

So ended Fox's rule of the stream.

Since he didn't know how to rule with care, he was not allowed to
   rule at all.

These stream creatures were all saved by just two tiny fellows,
   the little Pla Moo fish with the brave heart,
   and the small but clever rabbit who cared enough to help his
   water neighbors.

—A FOLKTALE FROM THAILAND

Where there is greed,
what love can be there?
   —SIKH WISDOM

Papa God's Well ❧

In this Haitian tale the caretaker of a well lets his power go to his head. We need to ask: Just who does our ground water belong to?

There was a time when the streams dried up.

There was a time when the rivers dried up.

The animals became very thirsty.

Some were even dying of thirst.

The animals held a meeting to talk about their problem.
"Perhaps we should call Papa God.
He put us here.
He ought to look after us.
Maybe Papa God can help."

So all of the animals began to call as loudly as they could.
"PAPA GOD!
PAPA GOD!
PAPA GOD!
WE NEED HELP!"

When Papa God heard that he came right away.
"You animals look terrible.
What on earth is wrong here?"

"Papa God, the streams have dried up.
The rivers have dried up.
We don't have any water to drink."

"Why didn't you call me sooner?" said Papa God.

> Don't you worry about this one minute more.
> They don't call me Papa God for nothing.
> I'll give you a WELL!"

Papa God sunk a deep well in the earth.
Papa God filled it with cool clear water.

> "I think I'll make this real pretty," said Papa God.

He planted mango trees all around the well, a whole mango grove.
It was a beautiful spot.

> "Now drink all you want, animals.
> This well is for YOU."

The animals rushed up and took turns drinking the cool water.

> "Thank you Papa God."
> "Thank you Papa God."
> "Thank you Papa God."

"You're welcome, animals.

> But just one thing about this well.
> Someone is going to have to stay by the well to guard it.
> I don't want wild animals making this water dirty.
> I don't want humans getting around here and throwing
>   trash in.
> This guard will have to stay by the well all the time.
> Do I have any volunteers?"

Lizard spoke up.

> "I'll do that, Papa God.
> I like water.
> Let ME guard the well."

"All right," said Papa God.

> "Lizard is the Guardian of the Well."

Papa God left and the animals all went home.
Lizard settled down to guard the well.
Next morning Lizard heard someone coming.

"Who's that walking through Papa God's Grove?"
Lizard called in his loudest, most official voice.

"It's me, Cow."

"What are you DOING in Papa God's Grove?"

"I'm coming to get a drink of water."

"Go AWAY.
        I'm GUARDING this well."

"I thought Papa God said we could all drink the water."

"Papa God put ME in charge.
        I decide who gets to drink.
        You might dirty the water with your muddy tail.
        Go away!"

"That's not fair," said Cow.
        "I wouldn't dirty the water with my tail."
Cow went away, very thirsty.

Soon Lizard heard another animal coming.
        "Who's that walking through Papa God's Grove?"

"It's me, Horse."

"What do you want?"

"I'm coming to get a drink of water from the well."

"GO AWAY.
        I'm GUARDING the well.
        You can't drink here."

"I thought Papa God said we could drink from the well.

"Papa God put ME in charge here.
        I decide who gets to drink.
        You might knock dirt into the water with your sharp hooves.
        Go away."

"That's not fair," said Horse.
"I wouldn't knock dirt into the water."
Horse went away, very thirsty.

Here came Dog down to the well.

"Who's that walking in Papa God's Grove?"

"It's me, Dog."

"What do you want?"

"I'm coming to get a drink of water."

"GO AWAY.
I'm GUARDING the well.
You can't drink here."

"But Papa God said we could drink the water."

"Papa God put ME in charge.
I decide who gets to drink.
Fleas might jump off your back into the water.
Go away."

"That's not fair," said Dog.
"I don't have any fleas."
Dog went away, very thirsty.

All of the animals were thirsty again.
They began to get sick and look just terrible.
Only Lizard had any water to drink.

One day Papa God came by.
"What is wrong with these animals?
They look terrible.
They look really thirsty.
Is something wrong with the well I gave them?"

Papa God walked over to have a look at his well.
Lizard heard someone coming.
"Who's that walking in Papa God's Grove?"

"It's ME."

"Who is ME and what do you want?"

"I've come to check on the water."

"GO AWAY!
This is PAPA GOD'S well.
You can't have any water."

Papa God stepped out from behind a mango tree.
"This IS Papa God."

Papa God was NOT happy.
"I told you to TAKE CARE OF the well.
I didn't tell you to OWN it.
This water was meant to be shared.
You are fired, Lizard."

Papa God called the animals.
"Come on in here and get yourselves a drink."

When the animals had all had a good long drink,
Papa God looked them over.
"I need someone else to guard this well.
This has to be someone who knows how to guard.
And this has to be someone who knows how to GIVE.
Papa God made this well
and Papa God wants EVERYONE to enjoy it."

Frog spoke up.
"I like water, Papa God.
I would guard the well.
I would share the water.
I would never forget that the well belongs to you."

So Frog was put into the well.

He sits today at the bottom of the well, still guarding it.

If you come near a well just listen.

You will hear Frog calling:

    "Papa God's well.

     Papa God's well.

     Papa God's well."

In Haiti there is a saying:

The well may belong to you, but the water belongs to GOD.

—A FOLKTALE FROM HAITI

More than we use, is more than we want.

—AN ENGLISH SAYING

CARING FOR OUR CREATURES

Two Women Hunt for Ground Squirrels ❧

In this poignant story a woman learns the pain felt by a mother ground squirrel when her young is wounded. From this small animal the woman learns that slaughtering the young is not a proper way to harvest game.

In summer time Athabaskan women go up into the mountains to
    hunt for ground squirrels.
This is a ground squirrel story.

Two women were hunting ground squirrels.
They went up in the mountains.
They built a little shelter to live in.
Every day they set their snares.
Every evening they checked them.
One woman caught big ground squirrels.
The other woman caught only small ground squirrels.

She was angry at the small size of those ground squirrels,
but she kept them anyway.
Just threw them in her basket to dry for winter food,
even though they were really too small to keep.
One day she saw a baby ground squirrel leg sticking out of her
snare.
"Now it's BABY ground squirrels!
Why can't I catch big fat ground squirrels like my friend?"
She was so mad she snatched that baby ground squirrel out of
the hole, snare and all, and threw it into the brush.
Then she started walking away.

She walked and walked, fuming with anger.
Suddenly she realized she was walking in a fog.
It got very cold.
She felt wet all over.
She had lost her way.
She wandered and wandered in the fog,
feeling wetter and damper every minute.

Then she heard a voice.
> "*Shighinidu . . . nigada,*
> Come here . . . come here.
> *Shighinidu . . . nigada,*
> Come here . . . come here."

She followed the singing
down the hill.
She felt her way with her walking stick.
Then she bumped into something.
She felt all around it.
It was a ground squirrel house!
A big hummock of grass.

From inside the house she heard the voice singing.
> "*Shighinidu . . . nigada,*
> Come to me . . . come to me.

Shighinidu . . . nigada,
  Come to me . . . come to me."

Then she heard,
  "Put your sleeve over your eyes,
    and lean your head against the house."

She put her sleeve over her eyes.
She leaned her head against the house . . .
and TUMBLED right inside!

She landed with a jolt.
That's what happened!

She sat up and opened her eyes.
She was inside a ground squirrel house.
A fire was burning in the center of the floor.
She sat down and tried to warm herself.
There was a mother ground squirrel sitting on the bed,
holding a ground squirrel child in her lap.
This mother ground squirrel had been singing,
  "*Shighinidu . . . nigada,*
    Come to me . . . come to me."

Now she began to rock her child and sing to it sadly.
  "My little ground squirrel, little child . . .
    Why can't you stand up?
    My little ground squirrel, little child . . .
    Why can't you stand up?"

The woman saw
a string was hanging from the ground squirrel child.
It was a snare, fastened around his waist.
Now she understood.
This was the baby ground squirrel she had heartlessly thrown
    away.
The woman went to the ground squirrel mother.
She gently removed the snare from the child's waist.

When she pulled the snare loose the ground squirrel child
   gasped,
"*Aaaaahhhh.*"

The ground squirrel mother looked at the woman.
   "You humans come here every summer.
   You are strangers.
   You don't know our ways.
   Please be more considerate.
   Do not be so cruel.
   Our children like to play.
   They keep running about.
   Don't be angry with them if they trip into your snares."

The ground squirrel child looked up at her.
   "*Nghuni Nghuni Ndaya!*
   Nghuni Nghuni Ndaya!"

"I understand," said the woman.

"Now, you may go," said the ground squirrel woman.
   "Put your sleeve over your eyes.
   Lean your head against the wall again."

The woman put her sleeve up over her eyes.
She leaned her head against the wall . . . and tumbled back
   outside.
The sun was shining.
The fog was gone.
She was standing in the meadow.

The woman started back along her snare lines.
In every snare she found a big ground squirrel.
From that time on, every summer
   this woman found big ground squirrels in her snares.

But if by accident a ground squirrel child was caught,
she carefully unwound the snare and set it free.
She had learned from the ground squirrel people how to behave.

That is what happened.
That is a ground squirrel story.

—A TANAINA ATHABASKAN TALE

&

Waga mi wo tsunette hito no itasa wo shire.

Pinch yourself and you will know the pain of others.

—A JAPANESE PROVERB

Gluskabe Traps the Animals 🐾

This Penobscot tale warns of the dangers of over-harvesting our wildlife. If Grandmother Woodchuck hadn't given her grandson such good advice, we might not have any fish or animals left to eat today!

Gluskabe lived with his grandmother, Woodchuck.
Grandmother Woodchuck raised him and taught him everything.
She taught him how to hunt.
She taught him how to fish.
She taught him all about how to make his living.

When Gluskabe grew larger he said,
"Grandmother make me a bow and arrows!
I want to hunt DEER.
I am tired of eating rabbit and fish all the time."

So Grandmother Woodchuck made Gluskabe a bow and arrows.
Off he went into the forest . . . and he came back with a DEER!
Grandmother was so proud of him.
"What a fine grandson!"

The next day he roamed off and killed a BEAR.
"What a great grandson I have!"

But Gluskabe wasn't finished.
"Show me how to make a canoe so I can hunt ducks."
So Grandmother Woodchuck showed him how to make a canoe.
Off he went paddling after ducks.
He came back with many ducks!

But then the wind came up and he couldn't paddle against it.
He tried hunting in the woods, but he couldn't catch any game.
So he went back home.

Gluskabe lay down on his bed and began to sing a wishing song.
He sang,

"I wish I had a game bag made of hair.
I wish I had a game bag made of hair.
I wish I had a game bag made of hair
So I could catch the beasts more easily."

So Grandmother Woodchuck took some deer hair.
She made a strong game bag of deer hair and tossed it to him.

But Gluskabe kept on singing.

"I wish I had a game bag made of hair.
I wish I had a game bag made of hair.
I wish I had a game bag made of hair.
Then I could catch the beasts more easily.
A STRONG game bag!"

So Grandmother Woodchuck took some moose hair.
She made a game bag of moose hair and tossed it to him.

But Gluskabe kept on singing.

"I wish I had a game bag made of hair.
I wish I had a game bag made of hair.
I wish I had a game bag made of hair.
Then I could catch the beasts more easily.
A STRONGER game bag!"

Grandmother Woodchuck pulled woodchuck hairs from her belly.
And she wove a strong, strong game bag of woodchuck hair.
Then she tossed this to him.

"Thank you, Grandmother Woodchuck!" said Gluskabe.

And off he went to hunt game.

In the woods, Gluskabe held open his game bag.
"Come quick, you animals!" he called.
"The world is coming to an end!
You will all perish!
Better run into my game bag here.
Then you will not see the world come to an end."

The animals all ran into his game bag.

He tied it up and carried it home to Grandmother.

"Look what I have here!
I won't have to hunt for game anymore.
I have ALL the animals trapped right here!"

Grandmother Woodchuck looked into the bag.
"Oh, my grandson, what have you done?
You must not take ALL the animals.
What will happen to our descendants?
There will be nothing left for them to eat.
No, grandson. You must let these animals go."

"Oh, well then . . . ." Gluskabe opened his bag.
"Go on home, animals.
The danger is over.
Run on home now."

Now Gluskabe noticed how hard his grandmother worked fishing.
He saw that she caught very few fish.
"I could help out," he thought.
"There must be an easier way to get fish."

Gluskabe built a trap clear across the river mouth.
He left an opening for the fish to get in.
Then he went out on the ocean and shouted as he moved about,
"The ocean is going to dry up!
Come quick, fish of every kind who hear me.

Swim into my river and you will be safe!
All who hear me hurry now!"

Then fish of all kinds swam into the river and entered his fish trap.
When all of the fish were in, he closed the trap and carried it home.

"Grandmother, you won't have to work hard at fishing anymore.
I have ALL the fish right here for you!"

Grandmother Woodchuck saw that fish trap teeming with fish.
There were so many that they were crowding each other out.

"Grandson, you have not done well.
All of the fish will be killed.
What fish will be left for our descendants in the future?
This is not the way to act.
You must let them go."

Then Gluskabe understood.
"You speak the truth, Grandmother.
I didn't think about the future."

"Okay, fish, the danger is over.
Swim along home now."
He opened his fish trap and let the fish go.

After that Gluskabe had some wisdom,
    though he still had much to learn.
How fortunate that he had a wise Grandmother Woodchuck
    to teach him!

—A PENOBSCOT TALE

&

Wu t'an k'ou fu erh tzu sha sheung ch'in.

Don't think immoderately of food,
and so slay living things without restraint.
—A CHINESE SAYING

The Mountain Goats of Temlahan ❧

A tale about human's cruelty to animals. A kind-hearted boy shows a better way to deal with wild creatures.

It was at Temlahan, on the Skeena River.
Many mountain goats lived near that place.
The young men would slaughter them by the scores.
They wanted only the fat from the goats' kidneys and intestines.
The rest of the meat and bones they left to rot.

Cruelty was the way of these young men,
and even of their children.
One day the hunters found a young kid by its dead mother's side.
They carried the baby goat home as a toy
and handed it over to the children.
But the cruel children considered this kid only a plaything to
     torture.
They threw it into the cold stream.
They laughed when it struggled out shivering.
They tossed it into the fire.
They laughed when it scrambled out scorched.

But one young man could not abide this torture.
He picked up the kid and rubbed red ointment on its burns.
Then he carried it off to the edge of the mountain and turned it
     loose.

"Here young one, go back to your mountain home.
And do not come again to the place of men."

Next day the Temlahan people saw a group of strangers approach.
These men looked strong.
They wore blankets of mountain goat skins.
They wore mountain goat headdresses.
The strangers invited the Temlahan people to a feast
at their home high in the mountains.

The villagers of Temlahan were pleased.
They prepared a feast for these strangers.
The Temlahan chief danced to show acceptance of the invitation.
But there was something strange.
The guests hid their mouths with their blankets when they ate.
They just shoved the food behind their blankets.
Later, when the feast was over and the villagers could not see,
the guests went outside and threw the food away.

A small boy told the people that he had seen the guests eating
        grass.
"They have their heads down on the ground.
Those people are eating GRASS!"
But no one listened to the child.

Next day the hunters followed the strangers high into the
        mountains.
There they were greeted by many men wearing
mountain goat headdresses and mountain goat blankets.
They were seated in a large house and the feast began.
All of the guests sat on one side of the house.
All of the hosts sat at the rear and sang for the dancers.
But the young man who had been kind to the kid was taken
        aside.
"Come sit by me," said a young man in a mountain goat blanket.
"Sit here by the house post.
If the dancing chief kicks the wall . . . hold on to me tight."

Now the chief began to dance.
He jumped over the fire.
He kicked!
He jumped over the fire.
He kicked!

He sang,

> "On the side of the mountain I lay my hoof.
> The Chief of the Mountain Goats kicks down the mountain!"

Suddenly he kicked at the wall of the house!
The wall fell outward.
He leaped and kicked at the other wall!
The wall fell outward.
The house shattered and everyone fell screaming into a deep
    abyss.
Right down the sheer mountain cliff they fell.

Only the hosts leaped to safety,
turning back into mountain goats as they leapt.

This was the revenge of the Mountain Goat People.
Revenge on those who had tortured and killed them so wantonly.

The young man who had shown kindness clung to his
    companion.
He alone did not fall.
But now he found himself on a ledge of the steep mountainside.
He would die yet, for there was no way down.
And he was clinging to a goat!
The goat said, "Do not be afraid.
I am the kid you saved.
See, there is a red mark on my back where you rubbed the
    ointment.

"I will lend you my mountain goat cloak and my mountain goat
    shoes.
With them you can leap down the mountain."

The young man put on the mountain goat cloak.
He put on the mountain goat shoes.
Then he looked down from the cliff.
He did not dare leap.

"Watch me," said his mountain goat friend.
The mountain goat put back on his cloak and shoes.
Then he leapt from the ledge . . . and landed easily on another.
From ledge to ledge he leapt.
"See, it is easy!
But as you leap you must say,
    'To the ledge!
    To the sand!
    To the ledge!
    To the sand!'"

So the young man put on the cloak.
He put on the shoes.
He gathered his courage
and he leapt!
    "To the ledge!" He landed on a ledge!
    "To the sand!" He landed on the sand!

And so down the mountain he went, leaping from ledge to ledge
until he reached the bottom.

There he took off the cloak and shoes,
and left them on a bush for his mountain goat friend.

But what sadness when he reached his village.
Only the women, children, and old men were left.
Every hunter had been killed in the vengeance of the mountain
    goats.

The young man gathered his people.
He told them of their cruelty to the Mountain Goat People.
He taught them never to slay mountain goats wastefully again.
He taught them never again to treat animals unkindly.

And to remember these lessons, the clan took as their emblem
the symbol of the mountain goat.

—A TSIMSHIAN TALE

&

Greed will take you where you would not be.

—A FULANI PROVERB

The Alligator and the Hunter ❧

If harvested properly, the game of an area will continue to be plenti-
ful. Here one man learns this lesson.

When a man was out hunting he came across an alligator far
    from water.
The alligator had crawled inland too far and become stranded.
The poor creature was so shriveled and dried that it could hardly
    speak.
In a cracked voice it begged the hunter for help.

The hunter kept his distance from the beast.
 But he did offer advice.
"Travel through the forest in that direction," suggested the hunter.
"There is a pool just a short journey away."

"No, please do not leave me," pleaded the animal.
"I am too weak to crawl even that distance.
 I shall surely die.
Come closer and let me talk to you."

Cautiously, the hunter came nearer.

"I know about you," said the alligator.
"You are a hunter,
 but the deer always escape you.
 Is that not true?"

It was true.
This hunter had very bad luck in the hunt.

"If you will aid me now," continued the alligator.
"I will tell you how to become a great hunter.
Will you do it?"

The hunter still feared to come close.
"If I were to carry you to the pool,
I would have to bind your legs so you could not scratch,
and tie your mouth so you could not bite me."

"Tie me up," said the alligator.
"Then you will not be afraid."
The alligator rolled over on his back and held up his legs to be
    tied.

So the hunter bound the alligator's legs with a cord.
He bound the beast's mouth tight.
Then he lifted the heavy animal onto his back.
After struggling under this weight for a long time,
he reached the river.
The hunter unbound the alligator and jumped back.

The alligator plunged into the river.
He sank to the bottom.
Then he swam to the top.
He dove to the bottom again.
And swam back to the top.
Three times the alligator dove and surfaced.
Then he sank again and stayed down for a long time.

At last the alligator swam back to the top and spoke.
"You have brought me to water and have saved my life.
Now listen carefully to my counsel.

"When you go back through the forest,
you will meet a small doe.

Do not kill the small doe.
She has many children yet to bear.

"When you go through the forest,
you will meet a large doe.
Do not kill the large doe.
She has children yet to raise.

"When you go through the forest,
you will meet a young buck.
Do not kill the young buck.
He has many descendants yet to sire.

"When you go through the forest,
you will meet an old buck.
This buck has lived long,
He has sired many young.
Now his time may end.
Aim your arrow at this buck.

"In the future remember to take deer as I have taught you,
and you will never lack for venison in your camp."

The hunter did just as the alligator had instructed him.
The young doe he passed by.
The old doe he passed by.
The young buck he passed by.
But when he saw the old buck,
he went close and took that buck.

From then on, the hunter took game just as the alligator had
    said.
And throughout his long life,
that hunter never lacked for venison.

—A CHOCTAW TALE

ả

The best horse needs a whip,
and the smartest person needs advice.

—A YIDDISH SAYING

The Curupira ❧

The Curupira is protector of the forests. Stories are told throughout Brazil, Paraguay and northern Argentina by hunters who have encountered this creature when they abused their hunting rights and took more game than was necessary for their own subsistence.

Some say the Curupira is a little man. Others say he looks like a little wild boy. He rides through the forest on the back of a wild boar. If he walks you cannot follow his tracks because his feet are on backwards! So if you try to chase him . . . you are really running away from him. And if you follow his tracks, you are going in the opposite direction from the Curupira. With his large, pointy ears, the Curupira listens for the sound of hunters or woodsmen in his forest. At the first sound of a *Chop!* on one of his trees he is off on his boar, hurrying to chase that man off. And when the Curupira is resting, hidden in his home in a huge forest tree, he loves to smoke his pipe! Here is a Curupira story.

Carlos had no luck whatsoever at hunting.
He went into the forest,
spent the entire day,
and came back with one small bird.

Finally he realized that if he wanted to find game,
he would have to ask favor of the Curupira.
Everyone knows that the Curupira is guardian of the animals.
He looks after them all.

Whenever game from his forest is taken,
the Curupira is there, watching . . .
checking to make sure that hunter does not abuse the forest.
Each hunter is welcome to take enough to feed his family.
To the Curupira that seems fair.
But more than needed?
That the Curupira will not allow.

This Curupira is a small fellow.
He loves to smoke his pipe and hang out with his animals.
When he wants to get around, he rides his pet wild boar!
Curupira's feet are placed on backwards.
This helps him trick the hunters in the forest.
They find footprints and follow them . . .
but the Curupira went the *other* way.

Carlos knew gifts please the Curupira.
He brought tobacco, and sweet honey.
He left these on a fallen tree, then went away.
When he came back . . . the gifts were gone.

Carlos had good luck hunting, now.
He came home with a paca and two birds.
From then on every day he took a gift.
From then on every time he brought back game.
But after a while, Carlos began to dislike bringing gifts.
 "Maybe, I could just leave the honey.
 I'd rather keep the tobacco and smoke it myself."
So Carlos left the honey for a gift.
And he still had luck in the hunt.

Then, after a while, Carlos began to think,
 "Maybe I don't really have to leave the honey
 I've become a good hunter.
 I don't need that Curupira's help anymore."
So Carlos stopped leaving even the honey as a gift.
Still, he continued to catch game.

About this time, a man came offering to buy things.
This man would pay money for the skins of some animals,
for the meat of others,
for the feathers of some birds.

"I can hunt," thought Carlos.
   "I could bring in lots of game.
   I could get this money."
So Carlos spent a long day in the forest hunting.
He found parrots, he killed them.
He found pacas, he killed them.
He found peccary pigs, he killed them.
He found deer, he killed them.
He found a rabbit, even that he killed.

Carlos laid his game out in a forest clearing to skin it.
He would pack out the meat first,
then the skins.
He was counting up the money he would make.

But just as he lifted his knife to slice open the first paca
a startling sight made him stop.

A tiny chick came marching out of the forest!
But this chick didn't have any feathers at all on it!
This was a totally NAKED chicken!

The chick glared crossly at Carlos.
It walked up and down looking at the dead birds and animals and
   shaking its head.
Then a voice boomed out of the forest.
   "Estefan! Are my animals there?"
The chick turned its little head toward the voice and called back,
   "Yes, Curupira! They are all here."
"Then bring them back to me!" ordered the voice.
The featherless chick marched right down the line of dead animals.
It stopped at the foot of each animal, pecked on it, and called:

"Pacas! Wake up! Curupira wants you to come!
Peccaries! Wake up! Curupira is waiting!
Deer! Wake up! Curupira wants you on your feet!
Parrots! Wake up! Curupira needs you!
Rabbit! You wake up too! The Boss wants you!"

As the little chick called . . .
each animal began to breathe and jumped onto its feet again.
The birds ruffled their feathers.
The animals stretched their legs.
Then, with the little naked chick in the lead,
the animals marched off into the forest towards the voice.
But before they left the clearing, the chick turned and stared at
    Carlos.

"Hey, Boss! What about HIM?"
There was a long silence.
Then the voice boomed out again.
    "Leave him for now.
    We'll take him NEXT TIME."
Then the little chick vanished into the forest
with the line of animals behind.

Carlos RAN from that forest.
He even left the territory.
They say he never hunted again.
But he left behind this story . . .
to warn others about the dangers of angering . . .
the Curupira.

—A FOLKTALE FROM BRAZIL

You should look what you can swallow,
and what can swallow you.

—A PROVERB FROM INDIA

# ALL THINGS
ARE CONNECTED

The Mosquito Extermination Project ❧

*This story reminds us of some contemporary governmental schemes.
The leaders thought they had come up with a good plan. But they
didn't think their project through to see what altering nature would
really cause.*

A city was once beset by mosquitoes.
They bit and buzzed until the residents could stand it no longer.
The ruler met with his counselors and considered the problem.
His chief advisor recommended a Mosquito Extermination Project.
They would bring in buckets of frogs and drop them all over the
    city.
These frogs would soon put an end to the mosquitoes.

Project Mosquito Extermination was soon put into effect.
Within days there was not a mosquito left in the city.
But a worse problem had ensued.
Now there were FROGS everywhere.
Frogs in milk jars. Frogs in wells. Frogs in cooking pots.

The situation was impossible.
The ruler met with his advisors and considered what to do.
His chief advisor suggested a Frog Extermination Project.
They would bring in baskets of snakes.
These would soon eat the frogs and the problem would be ended.

So Project Frog Extermination was put into effect.
The snakes were released into the city.
And within days, the frog problem was ended.

However, now there were snakes everywhere.
Once the snakes had finished off the frogs,
they began to eat the smaller animals.
And once those were gone, they began to swallow small children.

In the end the snakes were so numerous,
the people had to abandon that city and move elsewhere.

Project upon project.
Too many projects caused the city to be abandoned.

—A FOLKTALE FROM INDIA

৯▲

He fled from the rain
and sat down under the waterspout.
—A SAYING FROM SAUDI ARABIA

Gecko Cannot Sleep ❧

This Balinese story shows the interconnectedness of all things. It also points out that some natural nuisances just have to be endured.

One night the chief was awakened by a loud noise right under
his window.
"GECK-O! GECK-O! GECK-O!"
The chief got out of bed and leaned out the window.
There was Gecko.
"Gecko, what are you doing here?
It is the middle of the night.
Go home and go to bed."

"I can't sleep," said Gecko.
"The fireflies are flitting all around my house.
They are blinking their lights on and off . . . on and off . . .
You've got to make them stop.
You're the chief. Do something about it."

"I'll talk to the fireflies in the morning," said the chief.
"Now go home and go to bed."

Gecko dragged himself grumpily home.
"Geck-o . . . geck-o . . . geck-o . . ."

Next morning the chief called the fireflies.
"Is it true that you have been flashing your lights
on and off . . . on and off . . . all night long?
Have you been keeping Gecko awake?"

"Oh yes," said the fireflies.
"We have to blink our lights on and off all night.
 Buffalo leaves manure all over the road.
 Without our lights, people would step in the poop!"

"Why that is very thoughtful of you," said the chief.
"Just keep on doing what you've been doing.
 You can go home now."

So the fireflies went home.

That night at midnight the chief was awakened again.
"GECK-O! GECK-O! GECK-O!"

The chief leaned out his window.
"Gecko, go home and go to bed."

"But I can't sleep.
 The fireflies are still blinking their lights
 on and off and on and off . . .
 You said you'd make them stop."

"Gecko, the fireflies need to blink their lights.
 Buffalo leaves manure in the road.
 Without the fireflies' lights people might step in it."

"Then talk to Buffalo.
 You're the chief.
 Do something about it!"

Gecko went home so grumpily.
"Geck-o . . . geck-o . . . geck-o . . . "

In the morning the chief called Buffalo.
"Buffalo, is it true you have been dropping manure on the roads?"

"Oh yes.
 Rain washes holes in the roads every afternoon.
 So I fill them up with manure every day.

If I didn't to that, people would stumble in the holes and get
    hurt."

"That is very thoughtful of you, Buffalo.
Just keep on doing what you have been doing.
You can go home now."

So Buffalo went home.

That night at midnight the chief was awakened again.

"GECK-O! GECK-O! GECK-O!"

The chief leaned out his window.

"Gecko, will you please go home and go to bed."

"I can't sleep.
The fireflies are still blinking their lights
on and off and on and off . . .
You said you'd DO SOMETHING ABOUT IT."

"Buffalo fills up the holes that Rain washes out.
The fireflies light the road so people don't step in Buffalo's
    manure.
You'll just have to put up with the fireflies."

"Talk to Rain!
You're the chief.
Do something about it!"
Gecko went home grumbling.
"GECK-O . . . GECK-O . . . GECK-O . . ."

In the morning the chief called Rain.
"Is it true that you wash holes in the road every afternoon?"

"Oh yes.
I rain very hard every afternoon to make puddles for the
    mosquitoes.
If the puddles dried up the mosquitoes would die.

If the mosquitoes died there would be nothing for Gecko to eat.
So I rain hard every day."

"I see," said the chief.
"Rain, you may go home."

That night at midnight the chief heard,
"GECK-O! GECK-O! GECK-O!"
He leaned out his window.

"Gecko, go home and go to bed!"

"I still can't sleep.
The fireflies are blinking their lights
on and off and on and off . . .
You said you'd DO SOMETHING ABOUT IT!"

"Gecko, listen carefully.
If Rain doesn't rain every afternoon, there will be no puddles.
If there are no puddles, there will be no mosquitoes.
If there are no mosquitoes YOU, Gecko, will have nothing to eat.
Now what do you think of that?"

Gecko thought.
If the chief told Rain to stop raining,
Buffalo could stop filling the holes,
and the fireflies could stop flashing their lights...
but GECKO wouldn't have MOSQUITOES to eat.

"Gecko," said the chief.
"There are some things you just have to put up with.
Now go home and go to sleep."

So Gecko went home.
"Geck-o . . . geck-o . . . geck-o . . ."

He closed his shutters.
He closed his eyes.
And he went to sleep.

Outside the fireflies blinked
on and off and on and off . . .
Some things you just have to put up with.
—A FOLKTALE FROM BALI

ᏱᎭ

Vai mbua ite umuu.

There is no rainfall that doesn't bring mosquitoes.
—A KITUMBA PROVERB

The Golden Plow ❧

It helps to know where true value lies. Clearly, even vast riches are of little use unless we take into account our connection with the natural world. This is one of many tales of the wisdom of Solomon.

Solomon the Wise was once an advisor at a king's court.
Solomon's wisdom was respected throughout the whole country.
But there came a day when Solomon the Wise tired of royal life.
He walked out of the king's palace and took to the road.
No one knew where he had gone.

Without his advisor on hand, the king was afraid to make
    decisions.
He sent servants to try and find Solomon the Wise.
It was thought that he was wandering the country as a
    commoner.
But no one knew how to find him.

At last the king devised a test.
He had a plow made entirely of gold.
Then he sent his men to carry the plow throughout the
    countryside.
Everywhere they went they said,
"The king offers a challenge.
He wagers that no man in this country can correctly guess
    the worth of his golden plow."

Everyone came to try and guess the plow's worth.
But no matter what they guessed,
no one could come up with the correct answer.

At last they came to a poor man sitting by the side of the road.
He was eating a crust of bread and appeared to be a beggar.
Yet they asked him too,
"Would you like to guess the value of the king's golden plow?"

The man looked up. Then he looked down again.
"Do you really want to know what your plow is worth?"

"Yes, yes. We do."

"Well, I can tell you this," said the man.
"If it doesn't rain in May,
your plow isn't worth my crust of bread."

The king's men looked at one another.
Then the wisdom of his answer sunk in.

"This is surely Solomon the Wise," they agreed.

So they took him back to the king again.
And the country was once more ruled with wisdom.

—A FOLKTALE FROM RUMANIA

ᴈ♣

A tray full of money is not worth a mind full of knowledge.

—A LAO PROVERB

Botany in the Rain Forest ❧

*This author reminds us of the cyclical nature of our forests . . . a cycle
that humans often break.*

First, the nurse tree must die.
It must fall,
no matter slow or fast,
it must let go of sky,
lie forever lengthwise
in deadly moist embrace.
It must rot,
beautifully, pungently,
opening spores to seed.
Its straightline nurselings
will confound the innocent:
"What planted such a row
in these chaotic woodlands?"
There will be no trace.
After the final consummation,
the line of new trees will remain.
But first, and long before, the nurse must die.

—© LIZA HOBBS

OUR PLACE IN EARTH'S SACRED SPACE

Finding the Center 🌿

This Ojibway tale shows us the importance of keeping ourselves centered in the universe and achieving balance in our lives.

In the early years, the first humans were living on the island home that had been created for them on the back of a great turtle. For a long time, things went well there. But then a disease came, spreading sickness among them. Many people died. Among those who died was a young boy. The Great Spirit took pity on the child and called for Manabozho.

"Manabozho," said the Great Spirit, "take this boy back to the land of the living, and give the people there the medicine they need to live." The Great Spirit then handed Manabozho and the boy a bundle in which was tied up the wisdom and healing that humans needed in order to live healthy lives.

Manabozho set out with the young child. They went into a deep forest and at nightfall lay down to sleep. Manabozho had a dream. In the dream he saw an otter carrying a branch in its mouth. When Manabozho awoke, he knew he must search for an otter who would help him take healing to the people. Manabozho and the boy traveled for a long time; the boy was almost a young man when they came to a great lake. There, swimming playfully along the banks, they saw an otter. They called to the otter, but at first it paid no attention to them. They called and called, making noises such as an otter makes. At last, they got the otter to notice them. "You must come along with us, Otter," said Manabozho. "It is up to us to bring the healing ways to the people." And Manabozho convinced the otter to come along with them.

The three traveled on their long journey. They had many adventures and had to stop many times. The youth became a mature man. At last they came to a vast body of water and in it was the island home of the humans. Manabozho, the man, and the otter could see that the people looked sickly and weak. Many appeared to be starving and were wandering aimlessly around.

"They do not have the power of the four directions," said Otter. Otter dove into the water and swam close to the island, calling out to the people, "Look carefully at what I am doing." Otter swam to the east and then back to the center of the lake. Otter swam to the south and then back to the center. Otter swam to the west and then back to the center. Otter swam to the north and then back to the center. Otter showed the people how to always find the center, and how to be aware of the four directions, so that they could always be in harmony with the space they lived in.

Then Otter swam away and returned to its original home. Manabozho took the man back to his people, and they rejoiced to see him back among the living. Manabozho and the man took out the healing plants they had brought with them and began to make medicines to help the sick. They also showed the people how to find the balance between their bodies and their souls, so that they would fall sick less often. They shared the wise advice that was in the bundle sent by the Great Spirit:

Cherish wisdom.	Live peacefully.
Respect all life.	Honor your promises.
Be courageous.	Be honest.
Live moderately.	Share your gifts.

And for a long time after that the people lived in harmony with one another and with all that surrounded them.

—AN OJIBWAY TALE

❧

Ch'ŏngbang chich'uk handa.

He rushes toward heaven and toward the axis of the earth.
(Said of one who makes a hurry-scurry rush about.)

—A KOREAN SAYING

Avvaiyar's Rest ❧

We often feel that we are most holy when we are in a mosque, church, or temple. But the wise woman in this story reminds us that all of this earth is sacred space.

One evening Avvaiyar walked slowly past coconut palms while cows returned home for the night. The bells on their horns sang out as the light softened, threaded with red. Tired now, she searched for a place to rest and was pleased to find a temple.

Avvaiyar sat down, leaned back against a tree, and stretched her weary legs out. They pointed right toward the statue of a god.

Suddenly a young man, the temple priest, came running up to her. "Old woman," he cried. "Don't you see what you are doing? You are insulting the god by pointing your feet right toward him. Move them at once."

"My son," she said with a sigh. "I will be delighted to move them away from the god. Simply tell me in which direction there is no god, and there will I point my feet."

—A LEGEND FROM TAMIL NADU, SOUTH INDIA,
RETOLD BY CATHY SPAGNOLI AND PARAMASIVAM SAVANNA

❧

Even in a single leaf of a tree, or a tender blade of grass,
the awe-inspiring deity manifests itself.

—FROM *URABE-NO KANEKUNI*, JAPAN

Hidden Divinity ❧

This story suggests that our better nature may lie deep within ourselves and need some digging to discover.

They say there was once a time when all humans were gods. But those humans abused these rights so much that Brahma decided to take their divinity from them. All of the gods discussed this matter. They must hide the human's divinity in a place where the humans would never find it. Some suggested the depths of the sea. But they knew humans would dive even to the very bottom of the sea and find it. Some suggested the tops of the highest mountains. Others were sure that humans would climb even there. Perhaps in the heart of the earth? Humans were apt to burrow down and discover it there too. At last Brahma came up with a brilliant plan. "We will place human divinity deep inside of each human. They will never think of looking there."

The plan worked perfectly. Humans climb mountains, dive into the ocean, burrow into the earth. They race about from continent to continent, ever searching. But few think to stand still and search deep inside themselves.

—A LEGEND FROM INDIA

❧

Man knows much more than he understands.

—A JEWISH SAYING

NO THING IS WITHOUT VALUE

The Tailor's Jacket

It seems we throw things away nowadays the moment they become a bit worn. We could learn a lot from the tailor in this story. I have heard this story told in many delightful ways by other storytellers. This is my very short version, which any beginner can tell with ease.

A poor tailor was once given a bolt of cloth by a rich customer.
"You must use this for yourself," said the customer.
"You deserve a fine coat for the winter."

The tailor was overjoyed.
He set to work at once.

He measured and he cut,
and he measured and he cut.
Then he sewed and he sewed,
he sewed and he sewed . . .
and he made himself a fine new coat!

How the tailor loved that coat!
He wore that coat

and he wore that coat
and he wore that coat . . .
until the coat was all worn out.

The tailor could see that, even though it was worn in places,
there was still plenty of good material left in the coat.

So he measured and he cut,
and he measured and he cut.
Then he sewed and he sewed,
and he sewed and he sewed . . .
and he made himself a fine new JACKET!

The tailor was very proud of his new jacket.
He wore that jacket everywhere.
He wore that jacket,
and he wore that jacket . . .
until the jacket was all worn out.

The tailor looked at the ragged jacket.
And he saw that there was some good cloth still left there.

So he measured and he cut,
he measured and he cut.
Then he sewed and he sewed,
he sewed and he sewed . . .
and he made himself a fine new VEST!

How the tailor loved that vest!
He wore that vest everywhere.
He wore that vest,
and he wore that vest . . .
until the vest was all worn out.

Well, the tailor turned that vest this way and that.
And he saw that, yes, there was still some good material
    left there.

So he measured and he cut,
and he measured and he cut.
Then he sewed and he sewed,
he sewed and he sewed . . .
and he made himself a fine new CAP!

The tailor loved that cap!
He wore that cap everywhere.
He wore that cap,
and he wore that cap,
until even the cap . . .
was all worn out.

He turned the cap around and around,
and when he looked closely and he saw. . .
there was just enough good fabric left . . .
to make a button!

So he measured and he cut.
And he sewed.

And he made himself a fine new BUTTON!

Well, the tailor was proud of that button!
He wore that button,
and he wore that button,
until at last . . .
the button was all worn out.

The tailor was just about to throw the button away.
But when he looked closely at it he saw . . .
there was just enough left to make this STORY!

—A JEWISH FOLKTALE

❧

Az men ken mit ariber,
mux men arunter.

If you can't go over, go under.
          —A YIDDISH SAYING

Love the Weeds 🌱

Perhaps many of our difficulties with nature could be solved by following this gardener's advice.

Once the Mullah tried gardening.
He planted all sorts of seeds in his garden
and waited for the beautiful flowers to spring up and bloom.
A few did come up.
But alas, the garden was mostly filled with unsightly weeds.
They grew more quickly than the flowers.
And they too budded, bloomed, and distributed wafts of seed.

In desperation the Mullah made his way to the palace
to consult with the palace gardener.
This man was known for his skill with plants.

"I have tried everything," complained the Mullah.
"I pull them out.
I hoe them out.
I plant more flower seeds.
And what do I end up with?
Weeds! Weeds! Weeds!"

The gardener considered all this for a while.
Then he offered his wise advice:
"I think the best thing for you to do . . .
is learn to love the weeds."

—A FOLKTALE FROM IRAN

Yêu nên tôt,
ghét nên xêu.

Love makes everything look good,
Hate makes everything look bad.

—A VIETNAMESE SAYING

The Useless Tree ❧

This fable raises the question, "Is it ever useful to be 'useless'?"

While traveling in the Shang Hills, Tzu-ch'i came upon an enormous tree. The gnarled old tree spread so widely that a thousand chariots could shelter in its shade. Tzu-ch'i wondered, "What kind of tree is this? It must be unusually rare and valuable."

But when he examined its branches, he saw that they were too twisted to make straight boards. Its trunk was too knotted to yield smooth planks. And its roots were not solid enough to be used for coffins. When he tasted the leaves, his mouth was set afire. And when he sampled their odor, he found one whiff bad enough to drive a person mad for days.

"But of course," said Tzu-ch'i, "This is a useless tree. That is why it survived to grow so large."

It is thus with sages, too. Having mastered uselessness, they cannot be exploited.

—CHUANG TZU, CHINA (CIRCA 300 BC)

❧

Chih mu hsien fa, kan chin hsien k'ê.

A straight tree may first be chopped down,
a sweet well drained.

—A CHINESE SAYING

THE FOLLY OF HUMAN GREED

Too Much Sky 🌜

Piles of food taken yet left to rot. Does this sound familiar? This Nigerian folktale definitely echoes today's problems.

In days long ago, the sky was very close to the earth.
And the sky was good to eat!

People did not have to work at all.
They did not have to plant crops or hunt for food.
When they felt hungry,
all they had to do was reach up and break off a delicious piece of
    sky.
And that sky food was good, too.
It was simply delicious!

But people were greedy.
Even then....when they had all they wanted just for free.
They still were trying to see who could break off the biggest piece.

One person would break off a big hunk of sky and start nibbling.
His neighbor would look over and see that piece and think,

"I want MORE sky than he has."
That neighbor would break off an even BIGGER piece of sky.

Neither of those people could eat ALL the sky they had broken off.
So they would just eat until they were full,
and then toss the rest on the rubbish heap.

The sky looked at that rubbish heap.
It saw pieces of itself piled up there to rot.
It thought, "What a WASTE!
I sacrifice myself everyday for these humans,
and they just toss me on the RUBBISH heap!"

So he gave those folks a stern warning.
"If you do not STOP wasting my good sky food,
I will move so far away that you cannot reach me anymore."

After that the people tried to be more frugal.
They would just break off what they needed to eat for that day.
And if they broke off a little bit too much,
well, they would stuff it down anyway!
No one wanted to be caught tossing sky food on the rubbish heap.
The sky saw that their greed was still uncontrollable.
Now they were gobbling more food than they really needed.
But he let it pass.

Of course the people couldn't ALL control their greed forever.
One day a woman just rushed out without thinking,
and broke off a HUGE piece of sky.
She realized too late what she had done.
Her husband tried to help her eat it up.
But it was way too much for the two of them.
They called the other villagers,
but the huge piece she had broken off was too much.
Even the entire village could not eat it all.
At last they gave up and tossed the remainder on the rubbish
    heap.

When the sky saw that it became SO angry.
Sky flew right up into the air . . . higher and higher . . .
Now no one could break off sky food . . . ever again.

That is why now people have to work for their food.
But even in our day,
folks have not learned to live without taking more than they need.

—A BINI FOLKTALE FROM NIGERIA

&

El que mucho abarca, poco aprieta.

He who grabs much, grasps little.
—A MEXICAN PROVERB

Just a Little More 🐛

This retelling of a Portuguese folktale might remind us how easy it is to get caught up in greed and keep wanting "just a little more."

He walked each morning as the world turned once more towards the sun. His mind was at its clearest then; the air was pure and cool. While others slept, snuggled in their dreams, he made his way through the village streets. He headed towards the hills and the early morning glow that surrounded them. It was where the windmills worked and the sheep made their home.

As he walked along the ridge he let his thoughts come as they may. Sometimes they would float up on their own like bubbles in the water. And sometimes they would leave him quiet and still.

It was simply too early, too peaceful, to put the mind to work grinding ideas like the wind-driven millstones.

As king, the ruler of all he could see, he gave himself the precious gift of a day begun privately. It was this time of silence that gave him the strength to rule himself and the calmness to rule others. Up on the ridge that rimmed the village, the same wind that worked to make flour scrubbed his brain clean.

When the king had reached the top of his favorite hill, he spotted a shepherd sitting far below him. Watching the village sheep, the shepherd sat without moving on a large gray rock. "From this distance," laughed the king, "his sheep look like spring clouds floating on a green sky."

He watched the shepherd for some time and decided that the two of them should meet. After all, both men had the power of life and death over those they ruled. "I must visit him," the king observed. "Why, he even looks like a king sitting there on his throne of stone."

With that, the king set off to meet the shepherd. He worked his way down through the brush and stone, following the trail the sheep had made. His strong stride quickly ate the distance between them.

Down below on the rock, the shepherd was lost in his daily dream about all the things he did not have. He was so wrapped up in his wishes that he did not notice the king's approach. He was therefore quite confused and startled by a friendly "Good morning," which seemed to come from nowhere. He was so puzzled that, for a moment, he actually thought that one of his sheep had decided to speak! He soon found the source of the mysterious greeting as his eyes gathered in the sight of the smiling king. The shepherd, knowing very little but his sheep, failed to recognize the king. His simple eyes saw only a man; a man who would ease the loneliness of his day.

"And good morning to you," replied the shepherd cheerfully. "Would you like to share my bread and cheese?" Hungry from the long hike and curious about the shepherd's life, the king accepted the invitation. While the king ate the shepherd began to talk and talk and talk. It reminded the king of a landslide. His words, like pebbles, rolled and tumbled along, gained speed and freed others, until all slid together in one roar.

The king simply chewed his bread and nodded his head as if listening carefully even though the shepherd's words passed through his ears like wind through an open window.

Yet, the moment the shepherd finished chattering and began to speak openly of his beliefs, the king stopped eating and started listening.

"I'm not like other men," the shepherd said proudly, "I need very little to be happy, just a little more is all. Others wish in envy to have the great riches and power of the King. I simply wish for a little land and just a little more importance so others will respect me."

The shepherd paused and then began again, asking with passion, "Why must a king own it all? Look around us: This hill, the valley below us, even this rock we're sitting on—it all belongs to him. Why must he deny me just a little more happiness? He never uses this land; he's too busy getting fat on the sheep I've raised to miss any of it!"

The king put down the bread and cheese on the ancient rock and from his purse removed a shining coin. The shepherd refused payment, for he had given the meal freely. The king thanked him, but insisted that he examine the face etched forever on the coin.

The shepherd's eyes lowered as they focused on the coin. The king watched as the eyes and the light in them grew wide like a slowly opening shade. The shepherd refused to raise his head for he had recognized just whose portrait stared back at him from the gold coin.

"Perhaps I am getting a little too fat," the king said kindly. "It is rare to meet a man who truly knows what he wants and even more rare to meet a man of such simple needs. I wish to reward you with just a little more happiness. All the land from this rock that you can travel between now and sunset will be yours. But you must be standing here where you began exactly as the day ends. If not, you will not even own a single blade of grass."

The shepherd leaped to his feet like a hungry wolf, thanked the king and was off. Noting that the sun had already passed its highest point, the shepherd guessed he had three to four hours left.

"Plenty of time," he said as he reached the top of the hill. "I'll run along the ridge tops, for I've always loved the view." On and on he ran, ignoring the ache in his legs and the burning in his lungs.

Seeing a lovely stream that split the valley below him with its flow, the shepherd decided to run towards it. "I must have it," he said, "for what good is land without water?"

Since he was running downhill, he reached the stream quickly and began to race along it. He never paused for a drink, even though his throat was caked with the dust of his run. "No time to stop," he thought, "there will be plenty of time for that tomorrow."

Pushing himself faster, he soon reached the source of the stream, the point where it bubbled up from a crack in the ground. Suddenly, he realized he'd made a huge mistake: "What a fool I am! I've only run along one side of the stream. Why, anyone could come along to the other side and share my water!"

Crossing to the other side, he ran along its banks, with each step giving him just a little more land to call his own. He ran until the stream emptied into a little pond, and as he arrived he saw a fat fish jump.

"What a nice place to catch a meal, and I am awfully tired of lamb. I must have this too." He ran around the pond and as he neared his starting point his body refused to run further. Though his mind tried to reason with it, to convince it and finally even threaten it, his body didn't care.

Slowly, the shepherd made his way up the final hill to the ridge above the rock and the waiting king. With every bit of energy spent he had to stumble and crawl up that hill.

As he reached the top he saw the many spectacular shades of sunset glowing on the horizon.

The king looked up just in time to see the exhausted shepherd collapse. Saddened by the shepherd's failure to overcome greed, the king remarked to those who would miss him most: "Sheep, your king is gone." Running in circles for hours around the hills and fields, the shepherd must have covered miles of land. But in the end, lying there, he really needed only six feet. Or maybe a little more.

—A FOLKTALE FROM PORTUGAL,
RETOLD BY GREG GOGGIN

❧

Quien todo lo quiere, todo te pierda.

Who wants it all, looses it all.

—A MEXICAN PROVERB

The Origin of Puget Sound
and the Cascade Range ✒

A Northwest Coast Native American tale about greed. The argument in Washington State about who gets to own the water is continued today by politicians.

One time when the world was young, the land east of where the Cascade Mountains now stand became very dry. This was in the early days before rains came to the earth. In the beginning of the world, moisture came up through the ground, but for some reason it stopped coming. Plants and trees withered and died. There were no roots and no berries for food. The water in the streams became so low that salmon could no longer live there. The ancient people were hungry.

At last they sent a group of their people westward to ask Ocean for water.

"Our land is drying up," they told him. "Send us water lest we starve and die."

"I will send you my sons and daughters," Ocean promised the ancient people. "They will help you."

Ocean's sons and daughters were Clouds and Rain. They went home with the messengers from the dry country. Soon there was plenty of moisture. Plants and trees became green and grew again. Streams flowed with water, and many fish lived in them again. Roots and berries grew everywhere. There was plenty to eat.

But the people were not satisfied with plenty. They wanted

more. They wanted to be sure they would always have water. So they dug great pits and asked Clouds and Rain to fill them.

Clouds and Rain stayed away from their father, Ocean, so long that he became lonely for them. After many moons, he sent messengers to ask that his sons and daughters be allowed to come home.

"Let my children return home," he sent word to the ancient people. "You have enough water for the present, and I will see that you have enough in the future."

But the people were selfish and refused to let Clouds and Rain go. The messengers had to return to Ocean without his sons and daughters.

Then Ocean told his troubles to the Great Spirit. "Punish the people for their evil ways," prayed Ocean. "Punish them for always wanting more and more."

The Great Spirit heard his prayer. He leaned down from the sky, scooped up a great amount of earth, and made the Cascade Mountains as a wall between Ocean and the dry country. The long and deep hole left where the earth had been, Ocean soon filled with water. Today people call it Puget Sound.

The people east of the mountains are still punished for their selfishness and greed. Ocean sends so little moisture over the range that they do not have the plants that grow along the coast. But they still have the pits their grandfathers dug. They are Lake Chelan and the lakes south and east of it.

Ocean still grieves for his sons and daughters who did not come home. All day and all night along the beach he calls to them and sings his mournful song: *"Ah'tahlah'tahlah'! Ah'tahlah'tah lah'! Ah'tah lah' tah lah'! Come home! Come home! Come home!"*

—A QUINAULT-CHEHALIS-COWLITZ TALE

ба

Greed is never finished.
    —A SWAHILI PROVERB

POLLUTION RETURNS TO THE POLLUTER

Sharing the Wine 🌿

I have heard this story told in many versions—wine, beer, lemon-ade—the result of too much dilution is always the same. This story points up the importance of each person's contribution to society.

Several friends agreed to meet on the night of the full moon for an evening of wine and storytelling. Each person was to bring a jug of fine wine. The wine would all be poured into a bowl, and the friends would share the wine throughout the evening.

As each one planned for the evening, that person began to think, "Everyone else will undoubtedly bring fine wine to the party. There is no need for me to bring my best wine. I can just bring a poorer variety. When it is poured into the vat, no one will be the wiser." And so each planned in that way.

Then on the night of the party itself, each had another thought. "Once the wine is all poured together, no one will know *what* was poured in. Why don't I just bring a jug of *water*. One small jug of water will certainly not be noticed in that huge vat of wine." In this way *each* person made plans.

And so, on the night of the full moon, the friends poured their

110

"wine" into the vat, dipped their cups, made a pleasant toast, and downed . . a cup of water each!

Thus each learned: Pollution begins with *your* jug.

—A FOLKTALE FROM CHINA

ও⋅

Falsehood is common,
truth is rare.

—FROM THE TALMUD

Don't Throw Stones from "Not Yours" to "Yours" ❧

I have always loved the word play in this tale. It reminds us of the turn of the wheel of fortune. And speaks of the ill-advised actions of the polluter.

A rich man decided to make a garden in front of his house.
The land thereabouts was strewn with stones, and untillable.
So the rich man hired a crew of laborers to pick out the stones.
And to get the unsightly stones out of his garden,
he instructed the workmen to toss the stones over the garden
    wall.
There they landed in the public roadway.

A wise man passing by stopped to watch this.
He called to the rich man,
"Don't throw stones from 'Not Yours' to 'Yours'."

"Imbecile!" retorted the rich man.
"I throw stones from 'MINE' to 'Not MINE!'
These stones are on MY land.
I can do whatever I want with them."
And his workmen continued to toss stones over the wall.

The wise man shook his head and walked on.

But time is a wheel which turns all things.

In time the rich man's affairs worsened.
He lost money.

His property was sold.
The fine garden was no longer his.

One day, stumbling along the public roadway,
the former rich man stubbed his toe on a rock.
Looking around he saw that the roadway was covered with
    stones.
No one could pass without bruised feet.
Then, looking over the wall, he saw his own former mansion,
with its lovely garden—now no longer his.

Then he remembered the words of the wise man so long ago,
"Don't throw stones from 'Not-Yours' to 'Yours'."

—A JEWISH FOLKTALE

≈

In prosperity, think of adversity.

—A DUTCH PROVERB

PLANNING FOR THE FUTURE

The Tamarind Tree ❧

A tale of the importance of frugality and wise harvesting. Sometimes one must put off gratification now, in order to live well later.

In Thailand the story is told of two young friends who left their village in China and traveled to Thailand to make their fortune. When the friends arrived in Krungtep, the City of Angels (as Bangkok is known in Thailand), they made a pact. Each friend vowed not to spend money on meat until he had saved five hundred bhat. By vowing to eat only inexpensive vegetables, the friends could hope to save money much more quickly. And money saved can be invested to earn more money. The friends agreed to go their separate ways and meet again in five years to tell of their success.

Right away both friends found work as laborers. The pay was low, but each was confident that he would soon save enough to go into business for himself.

The first young man was true to his pledge. He ate only rice and a bit of vegetable at each meal. Everything that he earned, he saved. Soon he was able to buy a small cart and go about selling things. Still he did not spend money on meat for his meals. He con-

114

tinued to eat simply and save his money. And after a while he had enough to open a shop. Even then, he refrained from spending money, until at last he was a prosperous merchant. Now he could marry, purchase a house, and eat whatever rich foods he desired.

The second young man lacked this strength of character. He went without meat for a few weeks. By then he had saved a bit of money. He decided to splurge just once on a duck, as he was longing for a taste of meat. "Just one duck," he thought. "And then I will not yearn for meat again." But, of course, it was not long before he desired duck again. And so, as quickly as he was able to earn coins, those same coins dribbled out of his pocket. The years passed and he remained as poor as when he began. At the end of the five years he met his friend. Seeing the impoverished condition of his old companion, the wealthy merchant invited his poor friend to stay with him. He made a small hut in the garden available to his friend as a home and provided him with rice and salted fish. Pointing out a small tamarind tree, he told his poor friend that he could help himself to the leaves from that particular tree to flavor his food.

The poor friend was happy in these living conditions, but within a few days he went to the wealthy merchant and asked if there were another tree from which he could pick tamarind leaves. "The ones on that tree are all gone," he said. "Well, one leaf made my soup taste good, so I put two in and it tasted even better. Three made it taste best of all. Since I cook three times a day, I have used up all of the leaves on that small tree."

"Do you understand what you have done?" asked the wealthy friend. "You have stripped the tree. And now you have no leaves at all to flavor your food. If you had taken only a small leaf here and there now and again, the tree would have been able to continue to grow. After a while it would have been so large and strong that you could have picked as many leaves as you wanted. But at first, you should have used it sparingly.

"In the same way that you denuded this little tamarind tree, you stripped your own fledgling savings. Can you not learn the lesson of the tamarind tree and save now, so that you may enjoy a time of plenty in the future?"

The poor man realized his error. He stayed on at his friend's home. But now he began to save all that he earned. And after a while he, too, was able to invest in a business. In time he prospered. But he always kept in his courtyard a small tamarind tree . . . to remind him that leaves stripped too soon will never provide for the future.

—A FOLKTALE FROM THAILAND

ક્ષ

Isala kutyelwa siva ngolopu.

A person who will not take advice
gets knowledge when trouble overtakes him.

—A KAFFIR PROVERB

Emptying the Granary ❧

This tale reminds us that resources used must be renewed.

Late one winter a man came to his neighbor to ask a favor.
   "My own grain has all been used up.
     Could I borrow some from you until next year?"

The farmer had grain to spare, so he agreed.
   "Take what you need from that granary over there.
     All I ask is that you refill the granary next fall."

Next winter the man came again to borrow.
   "Take what you need from that granary over there,"
     said the farmer, pointing to the same granary.

But soon the man came back empty-handed.
   "That granary over there is empty!"

"If that granary is standing empty," said the farmer,
   "You must not have returned the grain you borrowed
     last winter."

—A EUROPEAN FOLKTALE

❧

Chaop chaduk.

One's own deed returns to oneself.

—A KOREAN SAYING

Planting for the Next Generation ❧

Few people bother to plan beyond their own life span. When my uncle began planting an orchard at age eighty the neighbors thought he was batty. But I remembered this story.

One day neighbors saw Nasreddin Hodja busily planting trees in the field near his home. Everyone gathered around and began to poke fun. "Whatever possessed you to start planting trees at your age? There is not a chance you will live to see these saplings mature!"

The Hodja just kept on with his work. After a while he straightened up and gave the assembled crowd a careful look. "Did it occur to you," he wondered, "that I might be planting trees for the next generation?"

And he stooped to his work once more.

—A FOLKTALE FROM TURKEY

❧

Kadang-kadang tiada makan buah-nga.

The man who plants a coconut palm
does not always eat the fruit.

—A MALAY SAYING

The Past and the Future ੩

A parable about past and future. The story suggests that rather than ruminating over the past, we should put our efforts into the future, as THAT is where we can still make a difference.

Two men on the road met a palm-tapper bringing home palm
    wine.
They called, "Give us some of your palm wine, Palm-tapper!"

But the palm-tapper looked at them carefully and said,
"Why should I give you from my palm wine?
Who are you?
What are your names?"

So the first man proudly proclaimed,
"My name is 'Whence-we-come'! I am most important.
Give of your wine to *me*."

But the second man argued,
"My name is 'Whither-we-go'! It is I who am most important.
Give of your wine to *me*."

And since the two began to argue,
the palm-tapper took them both to the judge to settle the case.
When the judge had heard their names,
he did not hesitate to give judgment.

"Whence-we-come, your name is good.
But your name is from the past.

There is nothing more for us to gain from the past.
So your name cannot be best."

"Whither-we-go, your name is from the future.
If we are to find a thing that is good,
we must find that thing there.
Your name is best."

So the palm-tapper gave of his wine to Whither-we-go.
It is true.
If good things are to come,
we must turn our attention to the future now.

              —A MBAKA FOLKTALE FROM ANGOLA

❢

Yoo bi, mu hwan.

He who has no care for the distant future,
will have sorrows in the near future.

              —A KOREAN PROVERB

THE WISDOM OF
THE ELDERS

Plowing Up the Road ≈

In times of need, it is often the old who can bring forth the wisdom to guide us. Many cultures have tales which remind us of this fact. This story is widely known in Europe and variants are popular in Asia and Africa as well.

There was a time, let us hope it is not our time,
when old people were considered an unwanted burden on
    the young.
An edict was sent from the king.
All old people were to be done away with.
And the sooner the better.

People hurried to comply with the king's orders.
But one man loved his father and refused to be so cruel.
Instead, he hid his old father in the basement under his
    farmhouse.
Every evening he brought food to the old man
and he spent the evenings visiting with him and keeping him
    company.

That very year a famine struck the country.

The crops failed, every one.

There was so little to eat that winter that the granaries were
     scraped bare.

By spring there was not even a grain left for seed crop.

Now the kingdom was in dire straits indeed.

But the old father said to his son,

"Do not worry.

We will get through this rough patch.

As soon as the spring rains soften the roads,

you must take your plow and dig up the track to our house."

The son thought his father's request strange.

But he did as he advised.

And within a week the road began to sprout with all sorts of
     crops.

There was wheat, and rye, and corn.

Even beans were growing up in the road.

"You see," said the old man,

"Every time the wagons haul grain or vegetables to market,

a few fall through the cracks or from the back of the wagon.

Those seeds needed only a good tilling and a spring rain . . .

and up they came."

When the king heard that crops could be had by plowing the
     roads,

he ordered all the people in the land to do the same.

Then he called the farmer to him.

"How did you have the wisdom to know this?"

"I did not," replied the farmer.

"But one who is older and wiser than I did."

When the king heard this, he understood what must have
     happened.

Suddenly he realized the folly of his ways.

"It is true," he acknowledged, "it is the old who have wisdom.
We may no longer need the labor of their bodies,
but we still need the wisdom of their age."
He decreed that the elderly should be held in respect from that
    day on.

So the farmer's father was brought from his cellar.
And the wise old man lived in dignity to the end of his days.

—A FOLKTALE FROM RUMANIA

৯

Chia yu lao, shih ko pao.

A family that has an old person in it has a jewel.

—A CHINESE SAYING

In Your Hands ❧

This brief tale appears in many cultures as part of a longer story. It is a nice anecdote to help us think of our responsibility to this earth.

A young man once thought to confound the elder of his village.
The old man was said to be exceedingly wise.
But the young man was certain his own wisdom exceeded
    that of the frail old man.
He had caught a young bird, and carrying this bird hidden in his
    hands,
he approached the older gentleman.

"Here is a riddle for you, old man,
"I have in my hands a bird.
Is it alive?
Or is it dead?"

He thought there was no way the old man could win.
If he guessed "dead,"
the boy would open his hands and release the living bird.
But if he guessed "alive,"
the young man would crush the bird in his hands.
When he opened them . . .
there would be a dead bird.

But the old man looked into the young man's eyes and said,

"The answer, my son, is in your hands."

—A FOLKTALE FROM INDIA

MANY VOICES BRING RESULTS

Frog and Locust 🐸

If only we all band together, what great things we might achieve.

Once it didn't rain for a whole year.
The grass turned brown and died.
Trees and bushes lost their leaves.
In the canyon bottom, where a lively stream usually flowed,
there were just a few puddles of water left.
And every day those puddles got smaller and smaller.

Living at the edge of one puddle was a frog.
The frog saw his puddle get smaller with each passing day,
and he knew that if it didn't rain the puddle would soon dry up.
And he would die!

But the frog knew how to sing a rain song.
So he sang to see if he could bring some rain.
The frog croaked,
 R-R-RAIN, R-R-RAIN, R-R-RAIN . . .

But his song wasn't loud enough to reach the top of the
    mountain,
and that is where the Rain God lived.
The Rain God couldn't hear the frog singing, and no rain came.

Not far from the frog's puddle was a bush,
and living in the bush was a locust.
The locust knew that if it didn't rain,
he wouldn't live through the summer.
So as he clung to the bush the locust buzzed,
    R-r-r-rain-n-n, r-r-r-rain-n-n . . .

But that song wasn't loud enough to reach the top of the
    mountain.
And when the locust saw that there were no clouds in the sky,
and it wasn't going to rain, he started to cry,
    Ee-he-he-he-he . . .
The frog heard someone crying, so he hopped over there.
He looked up and croaked,
    WHAT'S THE MATTER-R-R . . . ?
    WHAT'S THE MATTER-R-R . . . ?

The locust told him, "If it doesn't rain, I'm going to die!"

When the frog heard that, he thought about how the same thing
would happen to him if it didn't rain, and he started to cry, too.
    WAH-WAH-WAH . . .

But then the locust got an idea.
He thought, "When one person works all alone,
he doesn't get much done.
But when people work together, they can do a lot of work."

So the locust said, "Frog, maybe we should sing together."

The frog thought that was a good idea.
So they added their songs.

> *R-R-RAIN r-r-r-rain-n-n . . .*
> *R-R-RAIN r-r-r-rain-n-n . . .*

It still wasn't loud enough to go to the top of the mountain.
But it was loud enough to go to the next puddle up the canyon.
And living over there was another frog.
On the other side of the canyon, there were even more frogs.
They heard the frog sing and thought they would join in
and sing along with him.
They all sang

> *R-R-RAIN, R-R-RAIN, R-R-RAIN . . .*
> *R-R-RAIN, R-R-RAIN, R-R-RAIN . . .*

In the nearby bushes, and in the bunches of grass still growing
at the puddle's edge, there were also more locusts.
They heard the song and thought they'd join in too . . .

> *R-r-r-rain-n-n, r-r-rain-n-n . . .*

Soon all the frogs and locusts were singing,

> *R-R-RAIN, r-r-r-rain-n-n . . .*
> *R-R-RAIN, r-r-r-rain-n-n . . .*

It was a loud song! It went clear to the top of the mountain!

The Rain God heard the song.
He climbed up to the center of the sky
and gathered dark clouds all around him.
From the distant mountains he made the cool wind begin to blow.
Rain drops started falling. The rain fell faster . . . and faster.
It was a big storm!

The canyon stream filled back up with water.
The trees and bushes got new leaves.
The whole land came to life again.
And it was all because the frogs and locusts worked together!

And that's why it is to this day,
if one person's fields are dry and dying,
he doesn't go off by himself and sing for rain.
But all the people gather together.
They dance with one heart, and with one voice they sing.
And in that way they can always bring the rain.

—A PUEBLO FOLKTALE,
RETOLD BY JOE HAYES

The strength of one person does not go far.

—A BEMBA PROVERB

ONE PERSON'S DREAM CAN MAKE A DIFFERENCE

The Magic Garden of the Poor ❧

This story shows that one caring person can make a difference in the world. The story also has something to say in this age of homelessness. My thanks to Mary Lou Masey for discovering this wonderful Kazakh story and translating it into English. Here is the tale as I tell it.

There were two neighbors who became very good friends.
One man was a farmer.
He had a small plot of land but fertile enough to grow crops.
His neighbor had only a stony piece of land.
On his land he grazed sheep.

But one year a disease spread through the land,
the sheep all became ill and died.
The sheepherder went to his friend to bid him goodbye.
  "My sheep have all died.
  I have no way to earn a living on this stony ground now.
  I must leave this place.

Perhaps I can find some menial job in the city.
And if not, I will have to beg for my living."

But his friend the farmer would not let the sheepherder go.
"You will stay here.
I will give you half of my land and you can farm alongside
me."

"You cannot do that.
You have a small farm already.
You must not give half of it away."

"You are my friend and I want you to stay.
I am glad to share with you.
There will be less for me, yes.
But I will still have enough to survive.
You must accept."

So the sheepherder stayed.
The two friends farmed side by side for many years.
Then one day when the sheepherder was digging in his land,
he unearthed a pot of gold coins.
He ran to his friend the farmer.
"What luck! You are RICH!
Look what I have discovered!"

But the farmer would not take the gold.
"Nonsense. It is YOU who are rich.
The gold was found on your land."

"But when you gave me the land,
you did not know there was gold buried there.
You surely did not mean to give me all that was IN the land.
The gold is yours."

The two friends began to argue.
For the first time they could not agree.
At last they went to the village wise man for help in their dispute.

The wise man was teaching four students when they arrived.
When he had heard the problem he turned to his students.

"Here is a good case for you to discuss.
Neither of these men will accept the gold.
How would you resolve this?"

The first student said,

"It is simple.
The gold was found in the ground.
Neither man will claim the gold.
So put the gold back in the ground and forget it."

The wise man frowned and turned to his second student.

"And how would you resolve this case?"

"These men have brought the gold to you for a judgment.
What is brought to the court belongs to the court.
You should keep the gold."

The wise man's face turned dark.

"And you?" he turned to the third student.

"The gold was found in the ground.
The ground is in the kingdom.
The kingdom belongs to the Khan.
The gold therefore belongs to the Khan.
It should be taken to him at once."

The wise man's face turned black.

"What do you say?" he asked of the fourth student.

"The gold is here, yet neither of these men will claim it.
I suggest that the gold be used for the benefit of all.
With this gold there could be built a garden for the poor.
This garden could be filled with flowers to delight the eyes.
This garden could be planted with trees which would shade
the poor.

This garden could be planted with sweet fruit to nourish
    them.
This garden could hold cool pools of clear water.
From these the poor might drink without fear of becoming
    sick.
With gold such as this a fine garden could be created."

When the wise man heard this he smiled.
    "I like that idea."
He turned to the two men.
    "What do you say?"

"Yes. We like that idea also.
    Let this young man take the gold and fulfill his vision."

"Go to the city of the Khan," said the wise man.
    "Take this gold and buy the most wonderful seeds.
    Here is a plot of ground.
    Return and create your garden."

So the student set out.
It was a long, dusty trail to the Khan's royal city.
But he sustained himself on the way with his vision.
He saw before him that beautiful garden which he would create.

When the student reached the Khan's city,
he was surrounded by merchants shouting on every side.
The student felt confused and lost.
But, asking directions, he at last found the seed merchants.
He was just about to select his seeds when he saw a horrid sight.
A camel train was slowly winding its way down the narrow
    streets.
The camels were hung with live birds.
The poor birds were slung by their feet from the camels' sides.
Their feathers were caked with dust.

At every step the camels took,
the dangling heads of the birds thunked against the camels'
    sides.

The young man's heart turned when he saw this sight.
Without stopping to think he stepped in front of the caravan.
    "Where are you taking these birds?"

"These are for the table of the Khan," said the camel driver.
    "I have here the most rare birds in the kingdom.
    Some have been trapped on high mountains, some in distant
        jungles,
    others from far-off seashores.
    The Khan will decorate his palace with their bright feathers.
    He and his court will feast on their sweet meat.
    Some of these birds are the last of their kind.
    Only the Khan is rich enough to possess such birds!"

"I will buy these birds."

"Step aside," snorted the camel driver.

"No. I have gold.
    I will buy them."

The young man opened his bag and showed the gold.
It was more than even the Khan would have paid for the birds.
The camel driver took the gold and counted it.

The young student began to untie the birds.
One by one the birds spread their wings and flew off.
As they shook the dust from their wings and flew,
their bright feathers delighted the young man.

But some of the birds were too stunned to fly.
These he lay by the side of the road.
When all had been released, he began to stroke the poor sick
    birds.
All day he worked over them.

He gently removed the dust from their feathers.
He massaged their little bodies until their hearts grew stronger.

And one by one they, too, took to the air and flew away.

Then the young man turned back toward his village.
His heart felt so warm from this thing that he had done.

But as he came closer and closer to his village
he realized just what he had done.
He had spent the gold . . . the money that was to buy seeds.
Now there would be no garden for the poor.
The money had not been his to spend.

When he reached the spot where the garden would have been,
he sat down and wept.
    "How can I have done this?
      Now there will be no garden for the poor.
      And yet I had to save those poor birds."

A small bird was sitting nearby.
It cocked its head and listened to the young man.
Then the bird flew off.
Soon the air was filled with the sound of bird wings.
The young man looked up to find himself surrounded with birds.
Brilliant feathers filled the sky!
More and more birds glided down toward him.

"Do not cry," said the birds.
    "You saved us. Now let us help you.
      We cannot return the gold you spent.
      But we can help you with your dream for a garden."

The birds began to peck at the ground.
They began to roll stones out of the way and to prepare the soil.
And while the smaller birds were doing this task,
the largest birds flew off to distant lands.

There they filled their beaks with the most precious seeds they
    could find.
By the time they returned, the soil was ready.
Gently the birds planted the seeds.
Then they flew off to the stream to bring water for the plants.

Now smaller birds dug spaces for ponds within the garden,
while the larger birds flew high into the mountains,
bringing back cool, clear water to fill the pools.

Then a wondrous thing happened.
The birds began to fan the seeds with their wings.
and to blow on them with their hot breath.
Before the young man's eyes, the seeds began to sprout.
They grew quickly, emerging from the ground and reaching out
with their green shoots.
As he watched, the flowers budded and began to bloom.
Trees grew to full height right before his eyes.
They spread their branches, they blossomed,
their fruit grew and ripened,
and the trees hung with golden apples.
Not the kind of golden apple that you only admire,
but the kind from which you can eat and be nourished.

Word of the wondrous garden spread like wildfire.
The rich landlords jumped onto their horses and galloped
    to the spot.
They assumed that such a rich garden should belong to them.

But when the rich landlords galloped up they saw that
a fence of stone had risen around the garden.
There was an iron gate with seven locks.
And when the rich men arrived,
the iron gate swung shut.
And the seven locks locked themselves.
1-2-3-4-5-6-7 . . . the locks clicked shut.
The rich could not enter the garden.

One of the rich men stood up on his horse and reached over
the stone fence to pick one of the golden apples.
But the moment he touched the apple . . . *ZAP!*
He was thrown from his horse to the ground.

Another rich man reached for a fruit.
ZAP! He too was thrown to the ground.

After a while the poor began to arrive.
They had to walk to reach the garden,
so it took them some time to get there.
But when they came stumbling toward the gate,
1-2-3-4-5-6-7 . . . the locks clicked open.
And the iron gates swung wide.

The poor walked into the garden.
All day they strolled cool paths and rested on green lawns.
The flowers delighted their eyes and soothed their souls.
They plucked the golden apples from the trees and were
        nourished.
They drank the cool water in the pools and it did not
        make them sick.
In the evening they went back to their homes refreshed.

But some had no homes to go to.
These homeless folk lingered in the garden.

And then another wondrous thing happened.
As darkness fell the gates of the garden swung closed again.
And the seven locks fell into place.
1-2-3-4-5-6-7 . . . the locks clicked shut.
And all inside were protected for the night.

Then the golden apples began to glow with a gentle blue light.
The birds settled down in the trees and began to sing a sweet
        lullaby.
And the people lay down on the soft, cool grass and fell asleep.

Such is the Kazakh story of the magic garden of the poor . . .
which grew because of one young man.

—A KAZAKH FOLKTALE

&

Decide to do it, and the thing is done.

—AN ENGLISH PROVERB

AFTERWORD

The End of the Owls

This book has shown the thoughtful stories told by peoples around the world as they define their relationship with the land and its creatures. It is important that all of mankind realize very soon that we must work together to keep our planet alive. As an afterword I offer this sobering eulogy for an Earth which has been betrayed by mankind.

i speak for none of your kind,
i speak of the end of the owls.
i speak for the flounder and whale
in their unlighted house,
the seven-cornered sea,
for the glaciers
they will have calved too soon,
raven and dove, feathery witnesses,
for all those that dwell in the sky
and the woods, and the lichen in gravel,
for those without paths, for the colorless bog
and the desolate mountains.

glaring on radar screens,
interpreted one final time
around the briefing table, fingered
to death by antennas, floridas swamps
and the siberian ice, beast
and bush and basalt strangled
by earlybird, ringed
by the latest maneuvers, helpless
under the hovering firebells,
in the ticking of crises.

we're as good as forgotten.
don't fuss with the orphans,
just empty your mind
of its longing for nest eggs,
glory or psalms that won't rust.
i speak for none of you now,
all you plotters of perfect crimes,
nor for me, nor for anyone.
i speak for those who can't speak,
for the deaf and dumb witnesses,
for otters and seals,
for the ancient owls of the earth.

> —HANS MAGNUS ENZENSBERGER,
> TRANSLATED BY JEROME ROTHENBERG

ë&.

When you fall, I fall.
When you suffer, I suffer.
We are both in the same boat.

—OJIBWAY CHANT TO A SLAIN BEAR

Tale Collections with Ecological Themes: A Short Bibliography ❧

Earthtales: Storytelling in Times of Change by Alida Gershie (London: Greenprint, 1992).

Family of Earth & Sky: Indigenous Tales of Nature from Around the World by John Elder and Hertha D. Wong (Boston: Beacon Press, 1994).

Hidden Stories in Plants: Unusual and Easy-to-Tell Stories from Around the World Together with Creative Things to Do While Telling Them by Anne Pellowski (New York: Macmillan, 1990).

Just Enough to Make a Story by Nancy Schimmel (Berkeley, Calif.: Sister's Choice Press, 1992). See the bibliography, "Ecology Stories, Songs, and Sources."

Keepers of the Earth: Native American Stories and Environmental Activities for Children by Michael J. Caduto and Joseph Bruchac (Golden, Colo.: Fulcrum, 1988). See also: *Keepers of the Animals, Earth Tales, Keepers of the Night,* and *Keepers of Life* from the same publisher. This series of books is especially useful for the discussions and suggested classroom activities which accompany each story.

The Language of the Birds by David M. Guss (San Francisco: North Point Press, 1985). Poetry, folklore, and short essays.

Myths of the Sacred Tree by Moyra Cladecoot (Rochester, Vt.: Destiny Books, 1993). Focused more on symbolic and mythic content, rather than ecological. An interesting collection.

Spinning Tales, Weaving Hope: Stories of Peace, Justice & the Environment by Ed Brody, Jay Goldspinner, Katie Green, Rona Leventhal, and John Porcino of Stories for World Change Network (Philadelphia, Pa.: New Society Publishers, 1992).

Tales from the Rain Forest: Myths and Legends of the Amazonian Indians of Brazil retold by Mercedes Dorson & Jeanne Wilmot (Hopewell,

N.J.: The Ecco Press, 1997). Accompanying notes point out relationships to the forest.

The Way of the Earth: Native America and the Environment by John Bierhorst (New York: William Morrow, 1994). Discussion, with some short stories interwoven.

More Ecological Tales to Tell or Read Aloud ❧

In addition to the tales included in *Earth Care*, here are a few more excellent tales to share.

"All Things Are Linked" by Harold Courlander in *The Crest and the Hide* (New York: Coward, McCann & Geoghegan, 1982). All advisors but one agree with the king's every plan. That advisor says simply, "All things are linked." When the frogs are exterminated and mosquitoes then plague the village, his words are understood.

"Elsie Piddock Skips in Her Sleep" in *Martin Pippin in the Daisy Field* by Eleanor Farjeon (New York: Lippincott, 1937). With her magic jump rope and her incredible endurance, Elsie Piddock skips to win the fairy mound away from developers.

The Invisible Hunters or Los Cazazdores Invisible by Harriet Rohmer (San Francisco: Children's Book Press, 1987). A Miskito legend from Nicaragua about hunters who abuse their powers and overhunt with modern weapons.

"The Magic Box" in *The Way of the Storyteller* by Ruth Sawyer (New York: Viking, 1942). In this Italian folktale, Tonio inherits a box containing magic dust. If he shakes a few grains onto each corner of his field each day, he will prosper. As he makes his way about his fields daily, his eye is on everything that happens, and so his farm *does* prosper. On his deathbed, Tonio finds that there was nothing in the box but common sand.

"The Man Who Planted Hope and Grew Happiness" by Jean Giono, in *Sharing the Joy of Nature* by Joseph Cornell (Nevada City, Calif.: Dawn, 1989). True story of a man who spent the last forty years of his life planting trees. Single-handed, he reforested a section of southern France.

"Mouse Woman and Porcupine Hunter" in *Mouse Woman and the Mischief-Makers* by Christie Harris (New York: Atheneum, 1977). Porcupine

Hunter and his wife overhunt and are confronted by Great Porcupine, who teaches them a prickly lesson.

The People Who Hugged the Trees: An Environmental Folk Tale adapted by Deborah Lee Rose, illustrated by Birgitta Saflund (Niwot, Colo.: Roberts Rinehart, 1990). In this legend from India Amrita leads her villagers in hugging their trees until the ruler sees their value and agrees to let the trees stand.

"Slops!" in *Peace Tales: World Folktales to Talk About* by Margaret Read MacDonald (North Haven, Conn.: Linnet Books, 1992). And as a picture book, *Slop! A Welsh Folktale* by Margaret Read MacDonald, illustrated by Yvonne LeBrun Davis (Golden, Colo.: Fulcrum, 1997). An old man and woman discover they are dumping slops onto their fairy neighbors' house every day. They find a more sensitive way to handle their garbage.

"The Strange Folding Screen" in *Men from the Village Deep in the Mountains* by Garrett Bang (New York: Macmillan, 1973). A once-rich man, now living in poverty, decides to sell the mountain on his property. In a dream he is approached by the frog chief who asks him not to sell the land. If he does, it will be logged and the frog pond ruined. The man does not sell. In the night a marvelous painting of frogs appears on a sheet of blank paper in his house. Wet frog footprints lead up to the screen and the "painted" frogs seem almost lifelike. The screen is of great value in the art world.

"The Tiger" in *Family of Earth & Sky* by John Elder and Hertha D. Wong (Boston: Beacon Press, 1994), 156–57. A Jataka tale from India of the wood-sprite who asks that the tigers and lions be driven out of the forest because of their annoying stench. Unfortunately once these are gone, there is nothing to keep man from entering the forest and destroying it.

"The War Between the Sandpipers and the Whales" in *Peace Tales: World Folktales to Talk About* by Margaret Read MacDonald (North Haven, Conn.: Linnet Books, 1992). The sandpipers and whales each claim rights to the bay of their island. When each tries to destroy the habitat of the other, they see the folly of their ways.

"The Young Man, the Lion and the Yellow Flowered Swart-Storm Tree" in *Earthtales: Storytelling in Times of Change* by Alison Gershie (London: Green Print, 1992). This is not exactly an ecological tale, but it is a strange and touching story of a man and a lion which needs telling.

Proverb Sources ❧

Allan, Rev. C. Wilfrid. *A Collection of Chinese Proverbs.* New York: Paragon, 1964.

Brougham, A.D. and A.W. Reed. *Māori Proverbs.* Auckland, NZ: Reed, 1963.

Buchanan, Daniel Crump. *Japanese Proverbs and Sayings.* Norman: University of Oklahoma Press, 1965.

Elwell-Sutton, L.P. *Persian Proverbs.* London: John Murray, 1954.

Kītūmba, Vincent Mūli wa. *Sukulu Īte Nuta: The School with No Walls, Where Lifelong Lessons Begin.* Boise, Idaho: Vincent Mūli wa Kītūmba, 1977.

Kumove, Shirley. *Words Like Arrows: A Collection of Yiddish Folk Sayings.* New York: Schocken, 1984.

McDonald, Julie Jensen. *Scandinavian Proverbs.* Monticello, Iowa: Penfield Press, 1985.

Mieder, Wolfgang. *The Prentice-Hall Encyclopedia of World Proverbs.* Englewood, N.J.: Prentice-Hall, 1986.

Sellers, Jeff M. *Folk Wisdom of Mexico.* San Francisco: Chronicle Books, 1994.

Tê, Huynh Dinh. *Selected Vietnamese Proverbs.* Oakland, Calif.: Center for International Communication, 1990.

Theal, George McCall. *Kaffir Folk-Lore.* Westport, Conn.: Negro Universities Press, 1886.

Williams, Fionnuala. *Irish Proverbs.* Dublin: Poolbeg, 1992.

Windstedt, Sir Richard. *Malay Proverbs.* London, John Murray, 1950.

Yoo, Young H. *A Dictionary of Proverbs, Maxims, and Famous Classical Phrases of the Chinese, Japanese, and Korean.* Washington, D.C.: Far Eastern Research & Publications Center, 1972.

Tale Notes 🌱

The motif numbers in these notes refer to the Stith Thompson *Motif-Index of Folk-Literature* (Bloomington, Ind.: Indiana University Press, 1966) and to *The Storyteller's Sourcebook: A Subject, Title and Motif-Index to Folklore Collections for Children* by Margaret Read MacDonald (Detroit, Mich.: Gale Research, 1982). Type numbers refer to *The Types of the Folktale* by Antti Aarne and Stith Thompson (Helsinki: Suomalainen Tiedeakatamia Academia Scientarum Fennica, 1973).

Page 1: "Three Green Ladies" is retold from "One Tree Hill" in *Dictionary of English Folk-Tales* by Katherine Briggs (Bloomington, Ind.: Indiana University Press, 1971), 439–40. The story was collected by Ruth L. Tongue from a Derbyshire couple in 1935. Briggs observes that primroses are magic plants, especially in late May and June. Note the vestige of tree worship in this story. Motifs: F440.1 *Green vegetation spirit*; V11.1 *Sacrifice (gift) to tree*; F441.6.1 *Wood-spirits responsible for sickness and failure*; C518 *Cutting down tree tabu*; C43.2 *Tabu: cutting certain trees, lest tree-spirits be offended*; L13 *Compassionate youngest son.*

Page 8: "Treasure in the Vineyard" is based on an Aesop fable. See *Aesop Without Morals* by Lloyd W. Daly (New York: A.S. Barnes, 1961), 111, for a variant of this fable. Motif H588.7 *Father's counsel: find treasure within a foot of the ground. Sons dig everywhere and thus loosen soil of vineyard which becomes fruitful.* MacDonald's *Storyteller's Sourcebook* cites variants from Burma (bag of "gold" to be buried, contains rice, son obeys and prospers), Thailand (need two pounds of down from banana leaves grown by self for "gold" alchemy), Seneca (fox tells boy treasure is hidden by Jungies in field, spades up and mother plants corn), Upper Volta (clear plot of 10,000 square feet of bush and keep sweat in calabash, formula for wealth and happiness), Italy (shake dust from magic box on corners of field each day).

Page 10: "The Farmer and His Crops" is a Hmong folktale. For another ver-

146

sion see "Why Farmers Have to Carry Their Crops from Their Fields to Their House" in *Myths, Legends, and Folk Tales from the Hmong of Laos* (St. Paul, Minn.: Literature Department, Macalester College, 1985), 123–26. For another Hmong story about these crops see "Rice, Corn, Millet, Beans, and Wheat: Why the Five Grains Differ" in *Hidden Stories in Plants* by Anne Pellowski (New York: Macmillan, 1990), 79-80. This is Motif A1346.2. *Man must labor for a living: at first everything too easy. Full crops produce themselves, trees drop sugar, etc.* Stith Thompson cites sources from Greece, India, South American Indian, Seneca, and Jewish traditions.

Page 16: "Beast and Tree" is an original fable. While touring with my Mahasarakham University student storytelling troupe in Isaan (Northeast Thailand) in 1995, we met up with Jim Wolf, a retired educator and storyteller. Jim joined us on much of our tour and took to performing in tandem with Prasong Saihong, who translated while Jim told and both acted out the tale. Jim's telling of "Beast and Tree" was minimal in language, perhaps to make it easier on his translator. It involved much running about, snuffling, and caring for Beast's tree. I was touched by this parable and decided to write a poetic version of it which could be danced by my Bangkok friend Shirley Paukulis, who had previously interpreted stories to the accompaniment of my voice. Shirley danced the tree and Prasong danced the beast, while I read the tale. We presented this piece at Tellabration in Mahasarakham in 1996. It turns out that Jim Wolf learned the story from Adora Dupree and that she learned it from a book by James Dillet Freeman. When I finally located the original text, I found it amazingly different from the piece we were performing in Mahasarakham. James Dillet Freeman has given permission for inclusion of this new version, as well as his wonderful original story.

Page 19: "Who Is King of the World?" is an original short story by Unitarian theologian James Dillet Freeman. It appears in his book *Love, Loved, Loving! The Principal Parts of Life* (New York: Doubleday, 1974). It is reprinted here by kind permission of the author. This is the story from which "Beast and Tree," above, is derived.

Page 22: "Mikku and the Trees" is an Estonian folktale. See "How the Trees Lost Their Power of Speech" in *The Enchanted Wood and Other Tales from Finland* by Norma J. Livo and George O. Livo (Englewood, Colo.: Libraries Unlimited, 1999), 150–53. A more literary version of this tale is found in *The Sea Wedding and Other Stories from Estonia* by Selve Maas and Peggy Hoffman (Minneapolis, Minn.: Dillon Press, 1970). For other Estonian tales of supernatural helpers see *Estnische Märchen und Sagen Varianten* by Antti Aarne, Folklore Fellows Communications No. 25 (Hamina, Finland: Suomalaisen Tiedeakatemia Kustantama, 1918). I like to use this story for audience participation, improvising as I tell. I approach one member of the audience, ask what kind of tree he or she is, pretend to strike with my ax, and then ask why I should not chop them down. Most pick up on the refrain and call back "Stop! Stop! Don't cut *me*!" Motifs here are: C518 *Cutting down tree tabu*; D940 *Magic forests*; C51.2.2 *Tabu: cutting sacred trees or forests*; D1610.2 *Speaking Tree*; C600 *Unique prohibition. A person forbidden to do one particular thing*; and D1254.1 *Magic wand*.

Page 28: "Hold Tight and Stick Tight" is a Japanese folktale. A good version of this tale appears in the collection *Hold Tight, and Stick Tight* by Elizabeth Scofield (Palo Alto, Calif.: Kodansha, 1966). For a description of twelve more variants of this tale see *The Yanagita Kunio Guide to the Japanese Folk Tale*, edited and translated by Fanny Hagin Meyer (Bloomington, Ind.: Indiana University Press, 1986), 67–65. This is Motif Q2 *Kind and unkind*.

Page 32: "Spider and the Palm-nut Tree" is kindly contributed to this collection by Won-Ldy Paye and Margaret H. Lippert. Won-Ldy, who learned his stories from his grandmother, has put several of the tales of his Dan people into print in *Why Leopard Has Spots: Dan Stories from Liberia* by Won-Ldy Paye and Margaret H. Lippert (Fulcrum, 1998). Motifs are: W197 *Self-centeredness*; A2356.2.8 *Why spider has thread in back of body*; D482.1 *Transformation: stretching tree. A tree magically shoots upward.*

Page 35: "The Tiddy Mun" is a folk legend from a marshy area known as the Cars, in England's Ancholme River valley. "Cars" or "Carse" refers to a marshy land. A brief retelling by Katherine Briggs appears as "The Tiddy Mun" in *European Folk Tales*, edited by Lauris Bødker, Christina Hole, and G. D'Aronco (Copenhagen: Rosekilde and Bagger/ Hatboro, Pa.: Folklore Associates, Inc., 1963), 118–19, and in Katherine Briggs, *A Dictionary of British Folk-Lore* Vol. 1, Part B, (Bloomington: Indiana University Press, 1971), 377–78. My version is translated from "Tiddy Mun" in "Legends of the Cars" by M.C. Balfour, in *Folk-lore* 2, no. 2 (June 1891): 149–56. That version is heavy in dialect. I have tried to leave enough dialect to give the flavor in my version. Those who wish to tell this may want to consult both Briggs's abbreviated version and Balfour's original text. Balfour tells us he heard this "from an aged woman, a life-long dweller in these Cars, who in her young days herself observed the rite she describes . . . I tell these sto-

ries of the Cars of the Ancholme Valley exactly as told to me, lest in altering I might spoil them." "Tiddy Mun" includes Motifs F422 *Marsh Spirit*,
and Q552.10 *Plague as a punishment*.

Page 43: "The New Lake" is retold from *Chinese Fables and Anecdotes*
(Peking: Foreign Language Press, 1958), 23. This incident appears in *The
Records of Shao*. Notes say that it was related in two parts, the first by
Shao Po-wen of the eleventh century and the second by his son, Shao Po.
This is Motif J1934 *A hole to throw the earth in. Numbskull plans to dig a
hole so as to have a place to throw the earth from his excavation*. Stith
Thompson cites Jewish and Turkish versions of the story, MacDonald
cites versions from Mexico, Java, Scandinavia, and Turkey.

Page 44: "Fox Rules the Streams" is folktale from Isaan (Northeast Thailand). The story was translated into English by Supaporn Vathanaprida,
retold in a tellable format by Margaret Read MacDonald, translated into
Lao by Wajuppa Tossa and shaped through performance in Lao by the
Mahasarakham University Storytelling Troupe, then retold in English by
MacDonald. Motifs include: B479 *Small fish as helper*; K553.6 *Too dirty to
eat*.

Page 51: "Papa God's Well" is a folktale from Haiti. Versions of this story
appear in *Old Tales for a New Day* by Sophia Lyon Faha and Alice Cobb
(Boston: Prometheus Books, 1992), 91–95, and in *The Piece of Fire and
Other Haitian Tales* by Harold Courlander (New York: Harcourt Brace Jo-
vanovich, 1964). For more Haitian tales of Papa God see Diane Wolkstein's
The Magic Orange Tree and Other Haitian Folktales (New York: Alfred A.
Knopf, 1978). Motifs include: A2426.2.1 *Frog's croak*; W155 *Hardness of
heart*; W155.5 *Permission refused to drink from water tank*. Stith Thomp-
son includes one variant from India.

Page 57: "Two Women Hunt for Ground Squirrels" is an Athabaskan folktale. A wonderful version of "Ground Squirrel" is told by Antone Evans in
Dena'ina Sukdu'a: Traditional Stories of the Tanaina Athabaskans, com-
piled by Joan M. Tenenbaum (University of Alaska: Alaska Native Language Center, 1984), 148–55. The Dena'ina text is included there, along
with illustrations by Dale DeArmond. The version in this book is simplified
for beginning tellers. Advanced tellers should see also Tenenbaum's book.
The complete ground squirrel mother's song is given there as: *Shighinidu
nidaga/ sh-una yula/ una yula!*
    This tale includes Motifs: D2161.4.10.2 *Wound healed only by per-
son who gave it*; and M411.19.1 *Curse by wounded animal*. Stories of hu-

mans who visit an animal home and remove a knife or spear from a wounded child appear in Northwest Coast folklore as well. For example, the story of Naatsilane includes an episode in which the hero descends to the cave of the sea lions and removes a spear from the side of the sea lion chief's son.

Page 62: "Gluskabe Traps the Animals" is retold from "Gluskabe's Childhood," "Gluskabe Releases the Game Animals," and "Gluskabe Traps All the Fish" in "Penobscot Tales and Religious Beliefs" by Frank G. Speck in *The Journal of American Folk-Lore* 48, no. 187 (January–March 1935), 38–40. A retelling of this with useful notes is found as "Gluscabi and the Magic Game Bag" in *Wisdom Tales* by Heather Forest (Little Rock, Ark.: August House, 1996), 133–35. For those who wish to tell the story, I recommend Joe Bruchac's retelling in *Family of Earth & Sky: Indigenous Tales of Nature from Around the World* by John Elder and Hertha D. Wong (Boston: Beacon Press, 1994), 259–60. In this rendering Bruchac weaves some Abenaki language into the tale and follows with cultural information from his own Abenaki heritage. Motifs: J514 *One should not be too greedy*; J701 *Provision for the future.*

Page 66: "The Mountain Goats of Temlahan" is retold from "The Feast of the Mountain Goats" in "Tsimshian Mythology" by Franz Boas in *The Thirty-First Annual Report of the Bureau of American Ethnology 1909–1910* (Washington, D.C.: Government Printing Office, 1916), 131–35; and from "The Headdress of the Mountain Goat" told by Joshua Tsyebesa (Kitkatla, Gispewudwada Chief), recorded by William Beynon, 1916; "The Revenge of the Mountain Goats" told by Paul Dzius (Gitanmaax), recorded by Marius Barbeau, 1923; "Temlaxam and the Mountain Goats" told by Charles Mark (Gitseguekla), recorded by Marius Barbeau, 1923; all in *Tsimshian Narratives: Collected by Marius Barbeau and William Beynon*, edited by John J. Cove (Canadian Museum of Civilization, 1987), 246–52. A fine picture book, unfortunately out of print, is *The Mountain Goats of Temlaham* by William Toye, illustrated by Virginia Cleaver (Toronto: Oxford University Press, 1969).

Several interesting motifs were not included in my retelling: Charles Mark's version says that if you open the fur on a goat you will see the red ochre stripes of the medicine; Joshua Tsyebesa tells us that the hunter had been gone for ten years when he returned, though it seemed like only a day; two of the versions say that the people thought they were at a feast in a house on a prairie, rather than on a mountain. Music for the mountain goat chief's song is given in the Boas version. In three versions the hunter is instructed to call also "On the thumb" or "thumb-sticking-out" or "the-little-thumb" as he leaps down the cliff to safety. Interestingly, the variant recorded by Boas stresses that the bones and meat not used should have been burned. If the bones were left scattered on the ground the animals' sickness would grow worse and worse and they could not be cured. Thus people learned from this tale that they must always burn the bones and skin and any unused meat after a slaughter. This may, in fact, have been an important preventative in the spread of animal disease. Motifs: D334 *Goat transformed to person*; D114.4.0134 *Man transformed to goat*; B299.1 *Animal takes revenge on man*; B520 *Animal saves person's life*; B2 *Animal totems*. MacDonald cites five versions of this story under A1578.1 *Origin of family crests*.

Page 71: "The Alligator and the Hunter" is a Choctaw story retold from *The Choctaw of Bayou Lacomb, St. Tammany Parish, Louisiana* by David I. Bushnell, Jr., in the Smithsonian Institution Bureau of American Ethnology, Bulletin 46 (Washington, D.C.: Government Printing Office, 1909), 32–33. Motifs: B569 *Animals advise men*; M326 *Prophecy: success hunting*; B366 *Animal grateful for rescue from peril of death*; B375.2 *Frog returned to spring: grateful.*

Page 75: "The Curupira." The Curupira and Caipora are creatures of the forests of Brazil, northern Argentina, and Paraguay. Many variants occur in the Amazon basin, but the range of the creature's stories is much wider than this. My variant combines elements from "true" stories related in *The Enchanted Amazon Rain Forest: Stories from a Vanishing World* by Nigel J.H. Smith (Gainesville: University Press of Florida, 1996), 42–52, with "O Caçador e a Caipora" in *Contos Crioulos da Bahia,* narrated by Mestre Didi (Petrópolis, Brazil: Editora Vozes, 1976), 58–59. Additional information was taken from *Dicionario do Folclore Brasileiro* by Luis da Camara Cascudo (São Paolo: Edicoes Mehoramentos, 1979), 177–78, and *O Curupira* by Toni Brandão (São Paulo: Studio Nobel, 1998). Thanks to Suely Soares of Rio's storytelling group Mil e Umas for sharing her telling of this story and giving me copies of her sources. My version was inspired by her telling.

The Curupira is said to have backward feet, whereas the Caipora has normal feet. Other names for the creature include Caapora, and Caipira. The creature is small in stature, sometimes boylike in character, usually hairy and ugly. It rides on the back of a wild boar and loves to smoke tobacco. The Curupira is guardian of the animals and will do anything possible to stop wanton slaughter of its beasts. Motifs: F419.3 *Special spirit for each species of animal to act as its protector*; F551 *Remarkable feet.*

Page 79: "The Mosquito Extermination Project" is based on a folktale from India. It is retold from the *The Oral Tales of India* by Stith Thompson and Jonas Balys (Westport, Conn.: Geenwood Press, 1976). Motifs: J2100 *Remedies worse than the disease*; J2102.8 *Frogs to eat insects, snakes to eat frogs*; and J2103 *Expensive extermination of rodents.*

Page 81: "Gecko Cannot Sleep" is a folktale from Bali. This text is from a forthcoming picture book by Margaret Read MacDonald. In the winter of 1997 I was fortunate to visit Balinese storyteller Made Taro in Denpasar. Made Taro works with children twice weekly to teach them to tell the Balinese stories. It was a delight to share stories with his young students and enjoy their story performances in return. How fortunate we are that elder tellers are making the effort to train the young in this art. Anne Pellowski includes a variant of this tale in *The Storytelling Handbook* (New York: Simon & Schuster, 1995), 43–45. She heard the story in Jakarta in 1993. Motifs: J2102 *Expensive means of being rid of insects*; Z40 *Chains with interdependent members.*

Page 86: "The Golden Plow" is a Rumanian folktale. A brief version is found in *Rumanian Folk Tales* by Jean Ure (New York: Watts, 1960), 158–59. Motif F858 *Golden plow*. The notion of a golden plow appears both in Danish folklore and in tales from India, though without wisdom-test motif. Stories of the wisdom of Solomon are many. MacDonald Motif J1199.2* *Asked value of golden plow. Solomon-the-wise replies.*; H713.1 *How much is a golden plow (throne, crown, palace) worth? A rain in May.*

Page 88: "Botany in the Rain Forest" by Liza Hobbs is reprinted from *The Written Arts*, February 1990, 14, no.1 (Seattle, Wash.: King County Arts Commission), 38. © Elizabeth Hobbs

Page 89: "Finding the Center" is reprinted with permission of Friendship Press. It appeared as "How Medicine Came to the People" in *A World of Children's Stories* by Anne Pellowski (New York: Friendship Press, 1993), 121–23. Pellowski's tale notes tell us: "This is my retelling based on the texts in Henry Rowe Schoolcraft's *Algic Researches* (1839) and in his *Indian Tribes of the United States*, parts 1 and 5 (1853 and 1856). I also used *Ojibway Texts* collected by William Jones (Publications of the American Ethnological Society 7, parts 1 and 2, 1917 and 1919). A modern retelling may be found in *Mishomis*, collected by Edward Benton-Banai, available from the Red School House, 643 Virginia St., St. Paul, Minn. 55103." Motifs: Z71.2.1 *Formula: north, south, east, west (the cardinal directions).*

Page 92: "Avvaiyar's Rest" is reprinted with permission of Libraries Unlimited and the authors from *Jasmine and Coconuts: South Indian Tales* by Cathy Spagnoli and Paramasivam Samanna (Englewood, Colo.: Libraries Unlimited, 1999), 111. Spagnoli tells us that Avvaiyar was a sage who lived 2,000 years ago in Tamil Nadu. She wandered the land teaching people through songs and poems which are still shared today. Spagnoli notes that she heard this story told many times during her visits to Tamil Nadu.

Page 93: "Hidden Divinity" is a legend from India. This version is retold from an anecdote in "The Hiding of Divinity" in *Stories for Sharing: With Themes and Discussion Starters for Teachers and Speakers* by Charles Arcodia (Alexandria, New South Wales: E. J. Dwyer, 1991), 98.

Page 94: "The Tailor's Jacket" is a Jewish folktale and folk song. For an excellent version of this story see Nancy Schimmel *Just Enough to Make a Story* (Berkeley, Calif.: Sisters' Choice Press, 1992), 2. Doug Lipman has a delightful singing version of this story on his tape, *Tell It with Me* (Albany, N.Y.: A Gentle Wind, 1985), and I also enjoy using the picture-book version, *Something from Nothing* by Phoebe Gilman (New York: Scholastic, Inc., 1992). I have heard Robert Rubenstein of Eugene, Oregon tell this delightfully and involve the audience in all of the snipping and sewing at each turn of the story. Motif: J1115.4 *Clever tailor.*

Page 98: "Love the Weeds" is an Iranian folktale. For more stories of the Mullah see *Once the Mullah: Persian Folk Tales* by Alice Geer Kelsey (New York: David McKay, 1954), and see the works of Idries Shah, including *The Subtleties of the Inimitable Nasrudin* (Cambridge, Mass.: I S H K, 1983) and *The Exploits of the Incomparable Nasrudin* (Cambridge, Mass.: I S H K, 1987). For another version of this story see *Stories of the Spirit, Stories of the Heart: Parables of the Spiritual Path from Around the World* by Christina Feldman and Jack Kornfield (San Francisco: HarperSanFrancisco, 1991), 141-42. Motif: W25.2 *Minister always says, "It is for the best," when anything happens.*

Page 100: "The Useless Tree" is an anecdote recounted by Chuang Tzu, a Chinese sage of the third century B.C. For other versions see *The Essential Tao*, translated by Thomas Cleary (San Francisco: HarperSanFrancisco, 1991), 92–94, or *Chuang Tzu: The Inner Chapters*, translated by David Hinton (Washington, D.C.: Counterpoint, 1997), 58–61. For a storyteller's retelling, see Heather Forest, *Wisdom Tales* (Little Rock, Ark.: August House, 1996), 34. Motif: H659.11 *Riddle: What is most useful?*

Page 101: "Too Much Sky" is based on a Bini folktale from Nigeria. It appears in *In the Beginning . . . Creation Stories for Young People* edited by Edward Lavitt and Robert E. McDowell (New York: Odakai Books, The Third Press/Joseph Okpaku Publishing, 1973). An Ibo variant is given in Anne Pellowski, *The Family Storytelling Handbook* (New York: Macmillan, 1987), 36. Pellowski's variant comes from an autobiography, *My Father's Daughter* by Mabel Segun (Lagos: African Universities Press, 1965). Stith Thompson cites many sources for A625.2 *Raising the sky. Originally the sky is near the earth.* Versions come from Asian, Polynesian, African, and Latin American Indian sources as well as several from ancient sources (Egypt, Babylonia). Reasons for the lifting of the sky are varied. MacDonald gives one African American version under Motif A625.2.8* *People can break off pieces of sky to eat in the beginning.* This appears in Julius Lester, *Black Folktales* (New York: R.W. Baron, 1969), 381–41. This is also related to Motif A1346.2 *Man must labor for a living: at first everything too easy.*

Page 104: "Just a Little More" is a Portuguese tale. It is reprinted with kind permission of Greg Goggin from *Tales of the Old Country* by Greg Goggin (Berkeley, Calif.: Creative Arts Book Co., 1985), 27–32. Motif K158.7 *Deceptive land purchase: as much land as can be surrounded in a certain time.* Stith Thompson cites variants from Ireland, India, Iceland, and Frisia. In some cases the poor man actually wins the land, rather than losing it all to greed. See also Motifs W151 *Greed*; J514.2 *One should not be too greedy.*

Page 108: "The Origin of Puget Sound and the Cascade Range" is reprinted, with permission of the publisher, from *Indian Legends of the Pacific Northwest* by Ella Clark © 1981 Ella E. Clark (Berkeley, Calif: University of California Press, 1953), 25. Clark tells us "Clarence Pickernell, a Quinault-Chehalis-Cowlitz Indian from Tahola, Washington, told this legend in February, 1951. He had heard it from his great-grandmother. Pickernell pronounced the closing words rapidly, in a rhythm and with a hand movement to suggest the lapping of water against the shore." Motifs: A960 *Creation of mountains*; A962.4 *Mountains pressed together by God*; W151 *Greed*; A920.1.0.1 *Origin of particular lake.*

Page 110: "Sharing the Wine" is a Chinese folktale. For a longer version of this story see "Ten Jugs of Wine" in *Sweet and Sour: Tales from China* by Carol Kendall (New York: Seabury, 1979), 18–29. For a variant from the Bamum people of Cameroon see "The Feast" in Harold Courlander, *The King's Drum* (New York: Harcourt, Brace & World, 1962), 56–57. And yet another version appears as "The Jug of Water" in William White, *Stories for Telling: A Treasury for Christian Storytellers* (Minneapolis: Augsburg,

1986), 66–67. Motifs: K231.6.1.1 *Order to put a small vessel of milk into huge container. Shrewd group each by himself pours water thinking this will not be detected if the others pour milk.* Stith Thompson cites versions from India.

Page 112: "Don't Throw Stones from 'Not Yours' to 'Yours'" is a tale from the Jewish tradition. A version appears in Harold Courlander's *Ride with the Sun* (New York: Whittlesey House, 1955), 99–100. Courlander cites his source as the *Babylonian Talmud Baba Kama*, and *Tosefa Baba Kama*, chapter 2. A variant also is found in William J. Bennett, *The Moral Compass* (New York: Simon & Schuster, 1995), 113–14. MacDonald Motif: H599.10* *Don't throw stones from "not yours" to "yours."*

Page 114: "The Tamarind Tree" is a Thai folktale. Versions of this story appear as "The Story of the Two Chinese Friends" in *Burmese and Thai Fairy Tales* by Eleanor Brockett (Chicago: Follett Publishing, 1965), 163–70; also in *Folk Tales of Thailand* by P.C. Roy Chaudhury (New Delhi: Sterling, 1976), 37–40. Motifs: W216 *Thrift;* W15.6 *Ungrateful wanderer tears nut tree to pieces to get the nuts;* J701 *Provision for the future.*

Page 117: "Emptying the Granary" is a European folktale. Motif: J701 *Provision for the future.*

Page 118: "Planting for the Next Generation" is a Jewish folktale. This is Motif J701.1 *Planting for the next generation. Man who is planting tree told that it will never mature in his day. He is planting for the next generation.* Stith Thompson cites Turkish and Jewish sources for this tale. A similar story from Jewish tradition is told in *The Fable of the Fig Tree* by Michael Gross (New York: Henry Z. Walck, 1975).

Page 119: "The Past and the Future" is retold from "The Past and the Future" in *Folk-Tales of Angola: Fifty Tales with Ki-Mbundu Texts* by Heli Chatelain. (Boston and New York: American Folk-Lore Society, 1894), 247. The Ki-Mbundu text is in Chatelain's book. Motif: Z183 *Symbolic names.*

Page 121: "Plowing Up the Road" is a Rumanian folktale. A version appears as "The Land Where There Were No Old Men" in *Rumanian Folk Tales* by Jean Ure (New York: Watts, 1960), 169–71. For a nicely told variant see "Grandfather's Advice" in *Tales of Faraway Folk* by Babette Deutsch and Avrahm Yarmolinsky (New York: Harper & Brothers, 1952). This is Motif J151.1 *Wisdom of hidden old man saves kingdom.* MacDonald cites versions from Japan (old woman), the Congo (couple), Mongolia, and Slovenia. Stith Thompson gives sources from Ireland, Russia, Estonia,

Rumania, Spain, Italy, India, China, Jewish folklore and others. Under Type 981 *Wisdom of Hidden Old Man Saves Kingdom*, we find German, Swedish, Irish, French, Estonian, Lithuanian, Spanish, Italian, Rumanian, Slovenian, Serbocroatian, Russian, Turkish, Jewish, Chinese, and Indian variants.

Page 124: "In Your Hands" is a folktale from India. The tale appears in many variants around the world, most often as one riddle in a longer story. Recently it has become popular as a moral anecdote stressing the importance of taking responsibility for our planet's life. For example, see "The Hermit and the Children" by Susan Tobin in *Spinning Tales, Weaving Hope*, edited by Ed Brody et al. (Philadelphia, Pa.: New Society Press, 1992), 1. Motif H571 *Counter question. Riddles answered by a question that reduces the riddle to an absurdity.*

Page 125: "Frog and Locust" is a Pueblo tale. This story is retold by Joe Hayes in *A Heart Full of Turquoise* (Santa Fe, N.M.: Mariposa, 1988). It is reprinted by permission of the author. Motif A2426.4.1 *Frog's croak.* Stith Thompson cites variants from Japan, Angola, Liberia, Korea, and the Jewish tradition, but does not give specific reasons for frog's croaks. MacDonald cites two Vietnamese versions under Motif A2426.4.1.2.1* *Toad, wasp, tiger and cock go to complain to Jade Emperor about lack of rain. . . . Rain god agrees to rain whenever toad croaks.* One Chagga, African, variant is cited under Motif A2426.4.1.2.2* *In drought Rain Spirit responds when frogs dig deep holes and all croak.*

Page 129: "The Magic Garden of the Poor." This is a Kazakh folktale. It was inspired by "The Magic Garden" in *Stories of the Steppes: Kazakh Folktales* by Mary Lou Masey (New York: David McKay, 1968). Her sources were *Kkazakhskie Skazki V. I and II* by V.M. Sidelnikova (Alma-Ata: Kazakhskoe gos. Izd-vo khudozh, 1958, 1962), and *Pesni Stepei: Antologiia Kazakhskoi Literatury; Pod Redaktsiei Leonida Soboleva* (Moscow: Gosudarstvennoe Izdatelstvo "Khudozhestvennaia Literatura", 1940.) Motifs: D961 *Magic garden*; D1667 *Magic garden grown at once.*

Page 138: "The End of the Owls", a poem by Hans Magnus Enzensberger, is reprinted by kind permission of its translator, Jerome Rothenberg. This poem appeared in *New Young German Poets* (San Francisco: City Lights, 1959), 62–63, and in *The Language of the Birds* by David M. Guss (San Francisco: North Point Press, 1985), 322–23.

Acknowledgments

Thanks to Tuti Aranui, Kim Seuc, and Wajuppa Tossa for translation of proverbs. Thanks to the participants of the Storytell listserve (storytell@venus.twu.edu) for suggesting favorite ecological tales.

"Avvaiyar's Rest" is reprinted from *Jasmine and Coconuts* by Cathy Spagnoli and Paramasivan Samanna (Englewood, Colo.: Libraries Unlimited, 1999) with permission of the publisher.

"Botany in the Rain Forest" by Liza Hobbs is reprinted from *The Written Arts*, February 1990, Volume 14, no.1 (Seattle, Wash.: King County Arts Commission), 38, with permission of the author.

"The End of the Owls" is reprinted from *New Young German Poets* (San Francisco: City Lights, 1959) by kind permission of translator, Jerome Rothenberg.

"Frog and Locust" is reprinted from *A Heart Full of Turquoise* by Joe Hayes (Santa Fe, N.M.: Mariposa, 1988) with permission of Joe Hayes and Mariposa Press.

"Finding the Center" is titled "How Medicine Came to People" and is reprinted from *A World of Children's Stories* by Anne Pellowski (New York: Friendship Press, 1993) with permission of Friendship Press.

"Just a Little More" is reprinted from *Tales of the Old Country* by Greg Goggin (Berkeley, Calif.: Creative Arts Books Co., 1985) by permission of Greg Goggin.

"The Origin of Puget Sound and the Cascade Range" is reprinted from *Indian Legends of the Pacific Northwest* by Ella Clark (Berkeley, Calif.: University of California Press, 1953) by permission of the University of California Press.

"Spider and the Palm-Nut Tree" is published with the permission of its authors, Won-Ldy Paye and Margaret H. Lippert, © 1999 Won-Ldy Paye and Margaret H. Lippert.

"Who Is King of the World?" is reprinted from *Love, Loved Loving! The Principal Parts of Life* by James Dillet Freeman (New York: Doubleday, 1974) by kind permission of James Dillet Freeman.

157

Cultural and Geographic Index

২৯

As to your duty,
Start with that which is nearest to you.
—A JAPANESE SAYING